Something New

JOAN JOHNSTON

Previously published as *Fit to be Tied*

ISBN-13: 978-0-9912507-5-2.

This book is dedicated to my colleagues
in the Communication Department
at Barry University, Miami Shores, Florida
Sr. Marie Carol Hurley
Dr. Robert Jones
Dr. Peter Panos
Dr. Rise Samra
Dr. Timothy Simpson
in appreciation of their support and friendship.

PROLOGUE

He'd been watching her for an hour, and it was beginning to make her nervous. He was well over six feet, broad-shouldered, and lean-hipped. Forty-five minutes ago he'd lit his first cigarette, and now she'd caught him throwing away the pack. Otherwise, he hadn't seemed anxious, just attentive, as his gray eyes scanned her, then moved away to survey the other avant-garde art exhibits displayed in the small, but prestigious, Soho gallery. She'd started to approach him at last, but he was joined by another man, who looked harried, rumpled, and agitated, so she'd turned and edged away from the two of them. She felt the hairs rise on the back of her neck and shivered with anticipation. He was watching her again.

She'd been watching him for an hour, and it was beginning to make him nervous. He'd smoked half a damn pack of cigarettes in an effort to keep his mind off what he had to do, while he'd waited for George to arrive. The tall, slender blond appeared unperturbed by his study of her. Her eyes were as blue as the ocean on a sunny day, and looking into them had made his heart jump. That wasn't supposed to happen. He had work to do, and it was time he got to it. He didn't want to hurt her, but sometimes in his line of work, he didn't have any choice.

CHAPTER ONE

"I didn't expect her to be so feminine, not after everything I'd read about her. And her voice was so husky, as though she'd just finished drinking a whiskey straight up. I was right about what she does for a living, though. It's nothing a real woman ought to be doing, that's for damn sure."

"Come on, Matt, don't you think you're being a little hard on her?"

Matthew Benson ran a quick hand through his shaggy black hair. "I've been a critic for *Artist's World* a lot of years—"

"Long enough to have developed a less biased outlook toward female artists," George chided. "As your friend, not to mention your editor, I think you're letting your personal feelings about Jennifer Smith get in the way of your professional opinion. She hasn't allowed her gender to get in the way of her art any more than any other artist would."

"Except that in Jennifer Smith's case, her art is precisely aimed at making a *feminist* political statement. Women are as equal now as they're ever going to get. She's fighting a battle that's already been conceded."

"I know a lot of women who wouldn't agree with you."

"Not any I'd want to know—your wife excepted, of course."

George frowned and picked a piece of lint off the rumpled cotton shirt he'd ironed for himself that morning.

"You've been married to a liberated woman too long, old buddy," Matt said. "I like my women wide-eyed and long-legged, with lots of curves—"

"And dim-witted enough to fall for the lines you hand them."

Matt grinned, and two long slashes that God had probably intended as dimples appeared on either side of his mouth. "I don't demand intelligence, but I never said I don't appreciate it."

"What about Jennifer Smith?"

"What about her?"

"What are you going to say in your review about the body-art performance we saw tonight in Soho?"

"She certainly has the body for it," Matt quipped.

George grunted in disgust. "What about her art? You know how much clout *Artist's World* carries. Are you going to ruin her reputation as an artist because you don't agree with her politics?"

Matt's feet came down off his walnut desk. He pulled a cigarette from the pack in the breast pocket of his stiffly-starched shirt and lit it with the silver lighter he'd bought to celebrate his divorce. "I don't object to performance art in principle," he said. "But when a beautiful young woman like Jennifer Smith spends a year as a bum on the New York City streets and labels it *Be All You Can Be,* I think somebody has to start drawing some lines."

Matt turned abruptly and shuffled through the stacks of paper on his desk until he found a copy of *Focus on Art.* "I found this article on her by accident." He tossed the magazine to George, who grappled to catch it.

"Check out her next project. She plans to spend a month tied to a man by a ten-foot rope without touching him. Can you guess why?"

George shrugged. "No idea."

"To prove that the sexes can be separate but equal."

Matt grabbed the magazine back before George had a chance to locate the article and threw it onto his desk. "With the right man, she wouldn't last ten seconds in that situation."

"A man such as yourself?"

"Damn straight."

"Then why don't you volunteer for the job?"

"I've got better things to do with my time than spend it proving my point to some feminist prig."

"Sounds to me like a chauvinist pig and a feminist prig ought to get along together just fine," George said.

"Very funny." Matt leaned back in his swivel chair and settled the heels of his expensive Italian shoes on his desk.

"You still haven't told me what you think of the performance we just saw."

"You'll have to wait and read my review tomorrow morning," Matt said. "Now go home to your wife and let me get to work."

CHAPTER TWO

"I'm here to see Matthew Benson."

The *Artist's World* receptionist had strict orders from Matt to put off women such as the one who stood before her now: blond, beautiful and buxom, with pouting lips that begged to be kissed, and wide-spaced eyes that declared both innocence and feline intent. It was the woman's proud stance and exotic attire that caused the receptionist to pause for a moment before issuing the automatic rejection Matt had dictated.

The woman's cream-colored silk blouse buttoned all the way to the neck, but tatters of cloth that looked as though a cat had run its claws through the material were all that remained of the sleeves, which hung in ribbons from her shoulders. Her fitted black silk trousers had the same ragged effect from the knee down. This woman was clearly different from the norm. But orders were orders. "I'm sorry. Unless you have an appointment—"

"He'll see me. Tell him Jennifer Smith wants to speak

to him about his review of *Woman at a Party.*"

The receptionist winced as she placed the name. "It's nice to meet you, Miss Smith."

"That's *Ms.* Smith."

"Yes. So sorry." The receptionist glanced over her shoulder across the roomful of personal computers to a few private, glass-walled cubicles along the far back wall.

She punched out a number and spoke quietly into the phone, then said, "He'll see you. He's back in that far corner."

Jenny saw a hand waving in one of the cubicles and assumed it was Matthew Benson. Rotten chauvinist. Destroyer of artistic careers. Heartless creep. She crumpled the most recent copy of *Artist's World* more tightly in her hand and strode quickly toward his office, before she lost her nerve.

He met her at the door, and for a moment Jenny wasn't sure she could go through with what she'd planned. Then she remembered the harsh words he'd written. She lifted her chin, swallowed over the tight knot in her throat, and said, "Are you Matthew Benson?"

"Yes. Please come in, Miss Smith."

"It's Ms. Smith."

"Please come in, *Ms.* Smith," he repeated.

She narrowed her eyes at Benson's patronizing smile, then stared suspiciously at him when he held out a chair for her, as a true gentleman would, waiting for her to seat herself.

"I'll stand, thank you," she said. "This isn't going to take long."

"I hope you won't mind, then, if I sit?"

"Not at all." She watched him settle his rangy body comfortably in the swivel chair behind his desk. He looked somehow different from the shaggy-haired man who'd watched her so intensely at the Soho gallery, the man who'd made her heart race and put goosebumps on her arms.

She guessed he was her age, or maybe a little older—thirty-five? He'd rolled the sleeves of his oxford-cloth shirt up to reveal muscular forearms, loosened the top button of his shirt, and pulled the knot of his tie down. His shoulders filled the back of his chair from side to side, but his waist was narrow and his stomach was flat. She couldn't find one fault with his finely-honed male body, but then, she wasn't here to complain about his looks.

He met her gaze and said, "What's on your mind, honey?"

Jenny bristled at the condescending address and slammed the battered magazine down on his desk. The pages caught the edge of a Styrofoam coffee cup and sent it flying.

Jenny's warning cry came a moment too late. "Look Out!"

Even Matt's quick reflexes, as he jumped up to avoid the spilling coffee, weren't able to save his lightweight pleated pants from a dousing. He swore as he swiped at his trousers, trying to get rid of the excess coffee, most of which had landed in an embarrassingly personal spot.

Acting on reflex, Jenny grabbed a crumpled napkin from the desk and used it to pat him dry, even though he kept backing away from her as she worked. Suddenly he seemed to be choking, and Jenny looked up to see what else could have happened to the poor man.

He wasn't choking, he was laughing. Or rather, trying not to laugh. "If you'd wanted a chance to check me out,

Ms. Smith, I would have been glad to oblige. You didn't have to spill coffee in my lap."

Jenny looked down and realized that her hand was spread across the front of his trousers. The soaked napkin which, together with a thin layer of damp material, was all that separated her hand from his male flesh, wasn't hot. It wasn't even lukewarm. He'd never been in any danger of getting scalded.

Jenny dropped the napkin, which landed with a splat at Matt's feet, and backed around the desk, her hands balled into fists, her face fiery red. She was so upset she couldn't even enjoy the ridiculous sight the Great Matthew Benson presented to her.

He looked unruffled, but when she took another glance at his soaked trousers, she realized she'd evoked a response she hadn't intended.

Matt stood frozen for a moment, pretending a nonchalance he didn't feel. The truth was her touch had affected him more than he cared to admit, something that was rapidly becoming apparent. In an attempt to salvage what little dignity he could, he seated himself behind the concealing desk and leaned his forearms across it imposingly.

"All right *Ms.* Smith, say what you have to say and get the hell out of here, so I can go change my clothes."

The critic's condescending attitude immediately squelched any remorse Jenny had been feeling for the mess she'd made of his trousers. If he wanted to talk business, she'd talk business. She straightened to her full, five-foot-nine-inch height and said, "I think your review of *Woman at a Party* was unfair, especially the part where you define my support of women's rights as 'rehashing rotten eggs and spoiled corned beef.'"

"I'm entitled to my opinion."

Jenny glared at him. "Your opinion is biased."

"Your subject is outdated and stale. Like moldy bread. Or soggy crackers. Your art isn't relevant, *Ms.* Smith."

Was he an art *critic or a* food *critic*, Jenny wondered in disgust. She clenched her fists even tighter to avoid responding to Benson's disparaging remarks. After all, it was only one man's opinion, with *man* being the operative word. "You're wrong, and I'd like to suggest a way I can prove it to you."

"Lady, if you think you can change my mind about anything right now—"

"I want you to be a part of my next project." Jenny spoke quickly to get everything said while his mouth was still hanging open in shock. "If we spend thirty days together without touching—that is, if we prove my premise that the sexes can be separate but equal—I want you to print a retraction of your statements about *Woman at a Party.*"

He laughed. "You want *me* to be a part of your next project? The one where you're planning to tie yourself to some poor guy with a ten-foot rope for thirty days and dare him to lay a hand on you?"

Jenny swallowed hard as his eyes roamed her body appraisingly from head to toe. She felt stripped bare and reached up to check whether the button at her neckline was closed. It was. She patted the tight French twist that contained her silky blond hair. Every strand was safely in place. So what was he looking at? "You make it sound as though I'm issuing a challenge to the male sex. It isn't like that."

"Oh, yeah?"

"I simply want to make the point that men and

women have more to offer to each other than relief from hormonal needs."

"Hormonal needs?"

"Sex."

"And you think that if I'm tied to you for thirty days, I'll come around to your point of view?"

"Yes, I do."

Matt stood and leaned across the desk, putting himself nose-to-nose with her, his palms braced on the paper-strewn surface. "Hell will freeze over first."

Jenny found herself hard-pressed to hold her position, because now his face was less than a foot from hers. His gray eyes had locked with her blue ones, causing havoc with her pulse. She cleared her throat and said, "They say the polar ice cap is moving south a few inches every day."

Matt snorted his disbelief, shook his head, and stood up straight again, relieving the tension between them. "You seem pretty sure of my behavior, *Ms.* Smith. What about your own? What do I get if *you* can't keep your hands off *me* for the full thirty days?"

"If—and it's a pretty big if—I should be the one to touch you first, or if I should ask you to touch me, naturally I wouldn't be entitled to the retraction." Jenny's eyes narrowed. "But I wouldn't count on that happening. I assure you, I find nothing about you the least bit tempting."

Matt smiled, revealing a mouthful of perfectly straight, dazzling white teeth. "That's too bad. Some women find me quite attractive."

Jenny would have sneered at his arrogance, except she felt the same shiver of anticipation run through her that she'd felt when he'd watched her at the Soho gallery. "I assume you can control your sexual appetite for thirty days."

"I'm so certain I can control myself with you that, if I lose on that score, I'll print a retraction of my opinions about your art so fast it'll make your head spin. Not that I've agreed to this idiocy." He stepped around his desk and leaned back with his narrow hips against the edge of it, crossing his arms so his biceps bulged beneath the oxford cloth.

Unconsciously, Jenny backed up a step. She very carefully didn't look at the front of his trousers.

"You still have to give me one good reason why I should agree to tie myself to a woman for thirty days with the stipulation that we can't touch."

"Because you think you're right. And because you want to prove me wrong."

She was perceptive, Matt granted her that. He appreciated the ingenious simplicity of her appeal. "Even if I were inclined to take you up on this ridiculous proposition, there's no way I could get the time off to follow through with it."

"I spoke with your editor, George Taplinger, on the phone this morning, before I came here. Mr. Taplinger said he thought it was a wonderful idea, and that he'd be glad to give you the time off to do it. He said there were only a few exhibits you'd have to cover and, of course, he'd expect you to do a review and a short article on my project when it was finished."

"George agreed to this?"

"He did."

"He would," Matt muttered. He grimaced and asked, "How is this supposed to work? What happens when I want to pursue activities you're not interested in doing— Exercise? Movies? Football?"

"I'll come along with you," Jenny said. "Of course, when I teach my classes at the New School, you'll come along with me."

"We'd do everything together?"

"So long as we didn't need to touch, yes. With the understanding that we'll allow each other as much personal privacy as possible."

Matt smiled, but it was the feral look of a beast that knows its quarry is cornered. "You know, I'd almost be inclined to do this, if it weren't for some personal plans I have coming up this month, if you know what I mean."

"Would these plans entail spending time with another woman?" Jenny asked.

"Exactly."

"Our arrangement wouldn't have to interfere with that."

His eyebrows rose in disbelief. "No?"

"The prohibition on touching only applies to you and me. What other woman, or women, you choose to touch during the term of this project is your business."

"You won't mind?"

Jenny blushed. "I suspect there will be many times when we'll wish for more privacy than we have. I've resigned myself to it."

"For the sake of art."

"Yes."

Matt grunted. "This whole project strikes me as so much baloney."

Jenny rolled her eyes at the food metaphor.

He continued, "I know who I am and what I am. Who I am is a man. And what I am is attractive to women. I don't feel like spending the next thirty days fending you off."

Jenny stiffened. Did Matt Benson really believe what he was saying? Or was his male arrogance a ploy to get her to reject him as a partner for her next project? At that moment, she would have been happy to walk out the door and forget Matthew Benson existed. But after the review he'd just written, her choices were limited. If she wanted to convince him that the feminist statements she made through her art had validity, she needed him to come live for thirty days in her shadow. When he saw the world through her eyes, perhaps he'd better understand what she hoped to accomplish through her art.

And she needed that retraction. Her credibility with her peers depended upon it.

"Don't worry, *sweetie pie,*" Jenny said. "I want that retraction, and you don't want to give it to me. That ought to be enough to keep both of us at the ends of our rope. So what do you say, Mr. Benson?"

"Have you ever lived with a man, *Ms.* Smith?"

"Make it Jenny," she said. "And yes, I have."

"You don't find the situation you propose just a little, well, titillating?"

"I'm certain I could live platonically with a man, if that's what you're asking. I lived platonically with my husband for several months before our divorce."

Matt heard the bitterness in her voice. "Is that why you dislike men? Because your husband didn't desire you?"

"I don't dislike—" Jenny bit off her response. She felt the blood leave her face as she struggled for a suitable response to Matt's jibe. "I think it would be better if we left personal feelings out of this."

"He was a fool," Matt said.

"What?"

He sighed. "And so am I for doing this." He pursed his lips, then said, "All right, you've got a deal."

Jenny stood in stunned surprise for a moment before she realized she'd won the battle between them. "You'll do it?"

"Sure. Why not?"

"There's one more thing, Mr. Benson."

"Matt," he said treating her to his dazzling smile.

"Matt," she repeated, making her voice stern. "I've agreed to display my performance art at a different gallery for each of the next four weeks. We'll be traveling to San Francisco, Chicago, and Houston, then finish up here in New York the last weekend of the month."

"Damn! I should have realized—"

"You aren't backing out, are you?" she asked, making it a challenge.

At that moment, George stuck his head in the door. "How are you two getting along?"

"Just great!" Matt snarled. "Do you realize what you've gotten me into?"

"This decision was entirely up to you," George said. "But I take it Jenny persuaded you to participate in her project."

"Against all reason." Matt turned to Jenny. "Just tell me where and when to show up."

"My apartment, 7:00 a.m., day after tomorrow. We begin September 1 and finish September 30—if you can last that long."

He extended his hand. "Oh, I'll last, all right. Shall we shake on it?"

Jenny gave him her hand and felt a frisson of awareness streak all the way up her arm. She pulled herself free and, without a word, turned on her heel and headed for the door.

"I can't imagine why any woman would work so hard to prove she can be equal to a man," Matt said to her back.

When Jenny reached the door, she turned and said, "Neither can I. A woman who only wants to be equal to a man doesn't have much ambition." Then she was gone.

George chuckled, "Guess she got in the last word."

Matt sat down at his desk and put his feet up. "The game's just beginning. And as a famous sports*man* once said, 'It ain't over 'til it's over.'"

CHAPTER THREE

Jenny had a nervous stomach. And a sick head. And since she'd never believed in doing anything halfway, weak knees as well. It was 6:45 a.m. on September 1, and any moment, Matthew Benson was going to come through her front door. To say she was anxious was an understatement. Panicked was more like it.

She practiced the knot again, the one that was going to bind her to her nemesis for thirty full days and nights. If only Matt were a less obvious chauvinist. If only she weren't such a determined feminist. She wished she'd never considered using him as her partner in this project.

Jenny hadn't always been a feminist. In fact, the exact opposite had been true until she'd married Sam. Jenny had wanted nothing more from life than to marry and have babies. But when Sam hadn't earned enough money to support the children they'd both wanted, she'd gone out and gotten a job. She hadn't earned much when she'd started working at a small public relations firm in downtown Houston, but even that invasion of Sam's territory had been the beginning of the end of their marriage.

Due to circumstances neither of them could control, he'd lost his job just as she'd gotten her third promotion. He'd asked her to quit because he wanted—needed—to be the breadwinner. But by then, she was pregnant, and it was either keep working or lose her health insurance. Sam had told her to get rid of the baby, that they could have another one later on, when he could afford to pay for it. Jenny had been horrified.

It had been devastating to discover that her husband wasn't necessarily the Prince Charming she'd read about in fairy tales, nor even the hero glorified featured in romances. She hadn't gotten rid of the baby; she'd gotten rid of Sam. It had been agonizing to divorce him, and that hadn't been the end of the pain.

Her employer had demanded she quit her job when he found out she was pregnant, then refused to rehire her after the baby arrived. She might have won a lawsuit, but Jenny hadn't had the money or the emotional energy to sue. She suddenly found herself labeled a feminist and a liberated woman. She didn't care much for the labels, but she'd believed a woman ought to have the same opportunities as a man.

To her, that meant a woman had the right to be as successful, and as demanding of herself, as any man. It didn't mean she wasn't also a woman, with a woman's wants and needs. Which was why she was sorry she'd agreed to spend the next thirty days tied to Matt Benson. Because, unhappy as she was to admit it, Jenny was attracted to the man. The gravelly sound of his voice raised gooseflesh on her arms. His face would definitely not make milk curdle. And his body . . . Jenny had fantasies about sifting her fingers through his hair, letting her hands roam his broad shoulders, and—

"Hey, in there. Anybody home?"

Jenny started at the knock on wood—the object of her daydream had arrived in the flesh—and hurried to the door to start unlocking chains. In New York, you couldn't be too careful, so it was nearly a full minute before she opened the door to Matt Benson's devastating smile. A well-worn traveling bag was slung carelessly over his brawny shoulder.

"Here I am. What took you so long to open the door? Weren't you expecting me to show up?" he asked as he stepped inside.

"Yes, of course, but—"

"—in New York you can't be too careful," he finished with an understanding smile, eyeing the large selection of locks and bolts on Jenny's door.

She was appalled to find him so cheerful. She was never going to last thirty days if he kept smiling at her like that, creating those attractive creases in his cheeks. He was wearing jeans that fit him in all the right places and a white T-shirt under a black leather jacket that emphasized his broad shoulders. His hair was windblown and endearingly shaggy.

She wanted to touch—everything—and that was exactly what she couldn't do for the next thirty days. She followed the path of Matt's traveling bag as it came off his shoulder and slid to the floor. She was still staring at his black cowboy boots when he slipped off the leather jacket and dropped it onto the couch.

"Would you care to show me around first, honey? Or do we tie the knot right now?"

Jenny bristled at Matt's chauvinistic form of address. "Right now, we get a few things straight. The first is that I'm not your *honey.*"

"My mistake—Jenny."

Jenny was frustrated by his easy capitulation, since she could have used a rousing argument to ease the tension between them. She took a quick look at her watch. 6:48. "We have a few minutes before the project is scheduled to begin. It might be easier if I show you everything before we start. Follow me."

CHAPTER FOUR

Matt would have followed Jenny Smith anywhere. Her white cut-offs molded her fanny the way he wanted his hands to, and her generous breasts moved freely beneath the short-sleeved, black knit shirt she wore. How on earth was he going to keep his side of this bargain? Give him the chance, and he'd make her so hot she'd *beg* him to touch her, if he didn't go down in flames first himself.

She walked a step or two into the room, then gestured with outspread arms at a beige open-weave couch that was accented with nubby throw pillows. Nearby sat a bamboo swivel chair and a round, glass-topped table, with the latest art magazines arranged carefully on top. "This is the living area." She swept a hand toward the other side of the large room, where a wooden table and two wooden chairs stood guarded by a stainless steel stove, refrigerator, and sink. "That's the kitchen and dining room."

"I guessed that." He looked around the room again, noting the Oriental rug covering the hardwood floors. "No TV?"

"Do you watch much TV?"

"I've been known to catch a football game here and there, and the occasional women's mud-wrestling program."

Jenny wasn't sure if he was being serious or sarcastic. She responded with a neutral, "I see."

"Well?"

She crossed to a floor-to-ceiling oak unit along one wall and opened a set of folding doors. "The TV's in here."

Matt joined her at the cabinet and started opening more doors.

"What are you looking for now?"

"A stereo?"

"Sorry," she said. "Lost it in my divorce and never got around to replacing it. I have an AM-FM radio. Think you can find enough music on that to survive?"

"When in Rome." He shrugged nonchalantly, but she noticed him checking the titles of the books in her cupboard before she could close the doors.

Matt was confused by what he found. *Ms.* Smith had several books concerning women's issues, but she also possessed a large collection of romance novels. It seemed she spent half her time reading books attesting to how badly men treated women and the other half reading stories about heroes and heroines and Happily Ever After. He glanced at her and thought, *Will the real Jenny Smith please stand up?* Or, to give the devil her due, maybe she was a woman who could understand—and appreciate—both sides of an issue.

Jenny saw the two vertical lines between Matt's brows and quickly closed the doors on her small library. "Come on. I'll show you the rest of the place." She could almost feel his tall, lanky frame moving with her, as she passed through a doorway into the bedroom. She turned and discovered he was right behind her. She stepped back so quickly her foot caught on the area rug. As she fell, her breasts collided with his rock-hard chest. His arms naturally slid around her waist to keep them both upright.

Her blue eyes locked with his gray ones for a moment that seemed to stretch.

In a husky voice that she found incredibly sexy, Matt said, "Good thing I can still touch you. Otherwise, we might both have ended up on the floor."

Jenny shivered and gave a shaky laugh. "Yes. Very lucky." Her heart was beating a fast tattoo, and she realized she would have been perfectly happy to lay her head on his chest, slide her arms around his waist, and simply enjoy the feeling of being held in a man's arms. Instead, she took a step backward, forcing Matt to let go.

She turned her back on him, to avoid looking into his eyes, and said, "We'll be sleeping in here."

He walked around the bedroom like a lion inspecting a new den. Jenny tried to see the room through his eyes. She'd set up twin beds with a narrow rattan nightstand between them. The bedspreads were tan, and the lamp on the nightstand was the same navy as the area rug she'd tripped over, which partially covered the hardwood floor. The room was functional, considering what they had ahead of them over the next thirty days.

Matt hoped he didn't look as affected by their brief embrace as he felt. If he wasn't mistaken, *Ms.* Smith wasn't wearing a bra. He'd felt the soft warmth of her breasts against his chest as though she were naked, and his body had responded in a not unexpected way. Except, he hadn't expected *Ms.* Smith to turn him on. He angled his body away to hide his arousal and noticed something interesting.

There was nothing of a personal nature on the nightstand or the clothes chest except what he recognized—from having purchased a bottle for a former girlfriend—as a very expensive perfume. In a feminist's bedroom? He'd figured Jenny Smith would be into natural scents. Or maybe that was environmentalists. He casually strolled closer to her and took a deep breath to see if she'd sprayed some on. She turned abruptly and caught him sniffing, and he choked as he took a step back.

"Are you all right?" she asked.

"Fine. It all looks very . . . neat." No lint on the carpet. No dust balls in the corners. No layer of life on the furniture. No butts in the— *No ashtrays!* Matt glanced quickly around the room and said, "I don't see any ashtrays."

"I don't smoke."

Matt made his voice stern. "I do."

"Not in this apartment, you don't." She pointed to a sign on the end table: *Thank you for not smoking.*

It took Matt a moment to realize she'd put the sign in her bedroom. So, if *she* didn't smoke, who was she expecting to read—and heed—that message in her bedroom? He felt a moment of irrational jealousy and shook it off. "We need to discuss this."

Jenny looked at her watch. 6:52. "Talk fast. Patrick should be here any minute."

"Patrick?"

"The photographer."

Matt let that pass for the moment, because he wanted to address the smoking issue. "You knew I smoked when you asked me to participate in this project."

"Cigarettes aren't good for you."

"That's beside the point."

"You should quit."

"Do you want me to participate in this ridiculous project or not?"

"It's not ridiculous." When Matt opened his mouth to argue, Jenny realized she was running out of time and said, "All right. You can smoke. Outside."

He grimaced.

"It'll be fun," she said with a coaxing smile. "We can sit on the front stoop and people-watch."

Matt shook his head in disgust. Normally he could manage with only the occasional cigarette, but he'd been known to chain-smoke an entire pack in tension-fraught situations. He was pretty sure he was going to need a cigarette or two over the next thirty days. "I'm going to kill George," he muttered. But he didn't argue further. It was her home and her project, and he was willing—at least for the moment—to follow her rules.

Jenny opened the closet to show him the space she'd made for his clothes and he saw a riot of purple, orange, red, and green. Her clothes reflected the rainbow of color that had been missing in her navy and beige furnishings. He had no chance to ponder that anomaly before she opened the top drawer of a nearby chest and said, "I've cleared a drawer for you. "

Matt nodded his head toward the twin beds. "We certainly won't have to worry about bumping into each other at night, will we?"

"No, we won't." Jenny checked her watch. 6:55. "There's more to see, and we're running out of time." She wanted Matt to like her home, but she could tell he was disappointed about something. Surely he wasn't upset simply because she didn't have a stereo. Jenny's mouth twisted in a wry smile. Maybe he'd been expecting them to sleep in the same bed.

"Bathroom's here." Jenny opened a door off the bedroom to a small cubicle that contained a sink, commode, and tub, all white and spotlessly shiny. She showed him the hole she'd chiseled in the door frame so the rope that tied them together could run through it when the bathroom door was shut. She turned back to face him. "That's it. Any questions?"

"Did you stock anything to drink ?"

"There's water and soda." When his lips twisted wryly, she added, "There's also some beer in the fridge and wine in the pantry."

"I suspect I'm going to need something alcoholic before this is over."

Jenny smiled and conceded, "We both may." The knock on the front door sent them back to the living room. Jenny unlocked the door and welcomed Patrick Stuart with a warm smile.

The first thing Matt noticed was the pack of cigarettes in Patrick's breast pocket. "He's the one taking pictures?"

"Patrick will be photographing the project at intervals. He's doing a paper on social realism in art," Jenny explained. "My project qualifies as a contemporary example of the use of art to express social values."

She watched Matt shoot a look at Patrick and bristle, as though another dog had threatened to take his bone. Patrick was an exceptionally well-built, handsome young man. He had eyes as blue as the Caribbean, sun-bleached blond hair, and a smile that was blinding against his healthy tan. But as far as she was concerned, he couldn't hold a candle to someone with Matt's maturity, intelligence, and raw animal magnetism.

"Patrick Stuart, this is Matthew Benson, the critic for *Artist's World,"* Jenny said. "Matt, this is Patrick Stuart, my brightest and most talented student."

Matt stuck out his hand as though ready to take on the competition. "Hello, Patrick. Nice to meet you."

"The pleasure's mine," Patrick said. "I read your reviews all the time, and I respect your opinion, sir."

Jenny watched Matt's shoulders relax. It was hard not to like Patrick.

"Make it Matt," Matt said, smiling at Patrick.

Jenny glanced at her watch and felt her heartbeat ratchet up. 6:58. "Guess this is it. Patrick, get your camera ready." Jenny picked up the half-inch-thick white rope lying on the couch and turned to Matt. "Would you lift up your T-shirt so I can tie this around your waist?"

Jenny had carefully considered where to tie the rope and realized there was no place except their waists that would still allow them to change their clothes on a regular basis.

Matt reached down and pulled his T-shirt halfway up, exposing an abdomen ribbed with muscle.

Jenny had to reach with both hands to run the rope around his trim waist, and it forced her face against his chest. She couldn't breathe without inhaling the intoxicating scent of a piney male cologne. His cotton T-shirt was soft against her cheek, while beneath it, she could feel his rock-hard belly. She worked quickly, disturbed by the enforced closeness. She handed the rope from one hand to the other around his back and brought it to his stomach to tie *the knot.*

Jenny hadn't allowed herself to look at the skin he'd exposed when he'd lifted his shirt. When she tied the rope, she had no choice. His abdomen was striated with hard muscle, and the curly hair on his chest arrowed into a single line of downy black hair that disappeared into his jeans. He wasn't wearing a belt, and his pants had slid down on his hips, until they'd caught on his hipbones. If he was wearing any underwear, she didn't see any sign of it. Jenny shivered. Every time she moved the rope, her knuckles brushed his belly and he sucked it in, so his muscles rippled under her touch. Her hands felt clumsy, and her stomach fluttered.

Once she'd finished, she stepped back with a sigh of relief." All done."

"Thank God," Matt said under his breath when Jenny finally finished tying the knot around his waist. She'd known what she was doing, the little tease. If she'd glanced down, she would have gotten a pretty good idea of how successful she'd been. Well, two could play this game. He picked up the other end of the rope. "Your turn."

"I can do it," Jenny said, reaching for the rope.

Matt held it out of her grasp. "Turnabout's fair play."

Jenny dropped her hand, caught off-guard by the roguish look in his eyes.

"Any special kind of knot you want?" he asked.

"Whatever. Just make sure it's snug, but not too tight."

"Lift your shirt."

Jenny reached down and gathered the loose cotton folds of her shirt under her breasts. When Matt reached around her, his face was so close, she could feel his moist breath on her skin. She'd chosen the kind of cord used to hold back draperies, and the rope felt silky against her waist. The hairs on Matt's arm brushed against her, raising gooseflesh on her arms, and she quivered at the feel of his fingertips on her mid-riff when he secured the knot.

Matt couldn't believe how soft Jenny's skin was. He wanted to reach up under her shirt and cup her breasts in his hands, to take each of the nipples he could see tightening under the flimsy material into his mouth and suck them until she moaned. He wanted to taste her with his tongue until she shivered in his arms. He would do it all, he vowed. And before the damned thirty days were up.

He contented himself with brushing his knuckles across her abdomen and "accidentally" dropping his thumb into her belly button for a teasing caress. He took a quick look and found her eyelids heavy and her nostrils flared. She was all woman, whether she wanted to accept it or not. He had the next thirty days to prove it to her.

"There. All done," he said in a voice harsh with unfulfilled need.

They were both breathing heavily by the time he finished. Jenny only belatedly became aware that Patrick had been snapping pictures the entire time. She looked at Matt and got caught by a flash. She let her eyes adjust and checked her watch: 7:00 a.m. on the nose. "All right, Patrick. Time for one last picture. Step as far away from me as you can, Matt."

Matt took one, two, three steps away. Jenny had carefully measured the rope to be sure that after it was tied around both their waists it would still give them the desired ten feet of distance from each other. She'd walked off ten feet in her living room and knew it wasn't very far. It seemed even closer with Matt on the other end of the rope.

"Are you ready for a picture?" Patrick asked.

Jenny took a deep, calming breath. "Yes, I am. Matt?"

He fingered the rope at his waist as he said, "I'm ready."

Patrick adjusted the lens on his digital camera and snapped the picture. "I'd better get going. I want to print a few of these pictures before class today."

"I'll see you at nine," Jenny said, as she closed the door behind him.

"You teach today?"

"Half days Tuesdays and Thursdays," she said. "A class in art history and one on contemporary women artists."

"And you can make enough doing that to live?"

"I have another source of income."

She didn't elaborate, and he didn't ask. "How about a cup of coffee?" he suggested.

"I don't drink it," Jenny replied.

Matt groaned. "No coffee, either?"

"I've got tea."

"No thanks."

"We can go shopping later today and get some coffee and a coffeemaker," she offered.

"Swell."

"Can I offer you a toasted waffle?" When he stared at her aghast, Jenny stiffened her spine and said, "I don't like to cook, but mostly, I don't like to wash dishes. If you want a more elaborate breakfast, you're welcome to cook it and clean up after yourself."

"I'll take the waffle."

Since they were already as far from each other as the rope would allow, the moment Matt moved toward the kitchen Jenny was pulled along behind him. When he felt the rope stretched taut, he turned and cocked a questioning brow. "You coming?"

"I guess I don't have much choice," Jenny said with a shrug. It was done. They were tied by an umbilical cord for the next thirty days.

Matt sat at the kitchen table while Jenny took two waffles out of the freezer and popped them into the toaster.

"They smell like they're burning," he said a few minutes later.

"You want to cook?"

Matt shook his head.

"Then don't complain." When the waffles popped up, Jenny plopped them onto a plate and handed them to Matt with a butter dish and a plastic container of syrup. "Eat hearty."

Matt eyed the waffles suspiciously but found them surprisingly tasty.

"Who cooks for you at home?" Jenny asked, as she watched him wolf down his breakfast.

"I usually eat out. Or someone cooks for me."

Jenny had a feeling "someone" translated into "a woman I'm dating." "Why don't you learn how to cook?"

"I know how to cook."

"You do? Who taught you?"

Matt smiled sardonically. "My mother."

"Really?"

"She was a busy woman, much too busy to cook breakfast for the family. So she taught me how to do it."

"How big a family?"

"Five brothers and two sisters."

"I was an only child," Jenny said. "Were you the eldest?"

"Sure was."

"What else did your mother teach you?"

"I do a mean tub of laundry, I'm hell on wheels with a vacuum, and I can change a diaper in four seconds flat."

He was smiling when he said it, but somehow she knew he wasn't kidding. "So when did you become a male chauvinist pig?"

He laughed.

It was a booming sound, full of warmth and humor, that sent a frisson down her spine.

"You liberated women don't pull any punches, do you?"

"No. Are you going to answer my question?"

His face sobered. "When I got married." He frowned and said, "No. When I got divorced."

"Oh."

He played with the rope that lay on the table between them as he spoke. "My wife, Adrienne, was the consummate career woman. She chewed me up and spit me out like a used toothpick." He paused and ran a hand through his hair, rumpling it. "I was in and out of that marriage so fast, I didn't know what hit me. When we split, she took me for every dime I had. So much for liberated women being able to support themselves."

"I'm sorry," she said.

"It was a long time ago, and I learned my lesson. I won't be so quick to tie myself to another woman."

She watched to see if he'd realized what he'd said. He grinned ruefully. "Tie myself *permanently* to another woman."

Jenny took that to mean he was no longer interested in marrying. Well, neither was she—for her own reasons, which she had no intention of sharing.

"I'm done," he announced, sitting back in his chair.

"Done?"

"You can take these dishes away now."

This time it was Jenny's turn to laugh. "Remember me? The liberated woman? You can wash your own dishes."

"I figured I'm a guest, so—"

"We're both equals here," Jenny interrupted. "That means you do your fair share. I made the meal. You do the dishes."

"Is that the best deal I'm going to get?"

"It's the only deal you're going to get."

"In that case, excuse me." Matt stood, picked up his plate and silverware, and carried them to the sink to rinse them.

Jenny marveled at the play of muscles in his back and shoulders revealed by the tight T-shirt and wondered, not for the first time, how he stayed in shape. Maybe she'd find out over the next thirty days. His jeans hugged his taut buttocks, and she had a mental picture of her hands cupping them.

Abruptly she sat up straight, her face flushed with embarrassment. She'd been marginalizing Matt Benson, thinking of him as a sexual object.

Shame on you, Jennifer Smith!

I couldn't help myself.

The only reason Matthew Benson set foot through that front door in the first place is so you could prove that a man can treat a woman as more than a sexual object—and vice versa. Look at you! Only 7:42, and you're already ogling Matt Benson's buns!

You have to admit they're nice—

Jennifer!

All right. Geez. I'll start appreciating his male chauvinist mind.

Matt turned back to her, wiping his hands on a dishtowel. "How soon before we have to leave for campus?" He observed Jenny checking her watch—yet again—and realized how bound she was to the clock. Didn't she ever do anything without looking to see what time it was?

"I guess it wouldn't hurt to arrive a little early. My class is excited about the project, and they'll want to meet you before we get started. We can leave anytime you're ready."

He threw the dishtowel on the table. "I'm ready now."

Jenny picked up the towel and folded it, then walked over to rehang it on the rack by the sink. "Dishtowels go here when they're not being used."

Matt needed a cigarette. He squinted his eyes, scratched his ear, and asked, "Are you going to spend the next thirty days picking up after me?"

"Are you going to spend the next thirty days dropping things all over this apartment?"

Neither said anything for a moment, as the tension arced between them like an electrical current.

Matt took a deep breath and exhaled slowly. "I agreed to participate in your project, Jenny. I didn't agree to change who I am. If I drop something, you'll have to decide whether it bothers you more to pick it up or let it lie. I have no intention of tiptoeing around worrying about whether I've broken some unspoken rule. For the next thirty days, this is my home, too, and I'm going to treat it as such. Now, do you want to call this off right now, or do we go on from here?"

Jenny looked at her watch. 7:57. Three minutes short of an hour together and they were already at odds.

"Let's—"

Call it off right now, Jennifer. How will you ever be able to stand a whole month of that kind of highhandedness?

He isn't being so unreasonable, really. How would you feel if the circumstances were reversed, and you were staying at his place?

Can you imagine the chaos that must exist at his place?

That's beside the point.

That's exactly the point. How will your apartment look after he's spent thirty days dropping his undershorts beside the bed?

Jenny smiled at the picture that thought conjured.

"All right, Matt. I'll try not to pick up after you. At least I won't criticize you, if I do. Will that satisfy you?"

"Sounds good to me."

She couldn't wait to see that pile of undershorts beside his bed.

CHAPTER FIVE

Jenny's students were as excited to be able to witness her performance art project as she'd thought they would be, and they spent half the class asking Matt questions about what it was like to be an art critic. Jenny was impressed by how astutely he answered and had to admit he hadn't gotten where he was by accident.

When she began her lecture, he sat down in a chair near the podium to be out of the way. Jenny hadn't realized how much she paced in the classroom, or how often she moved in close to her students to make a point. Her rope only gave her three short strides before she was pulled up short. The third time she found herself stopped so abruptly, Matt grinned ruefully at her, set his chair aside, and stood near the blackboard, ready to move when she did.

When the class was over and her students had left, Jenny turned to him and said a simple but heartfelt, "Thank you."

"I'm sure you would have done the same for me. You were doing such a good job teaching, I hated to be in the way."

Jenny turned away to conceal her blush of pleasure at the compliment.

Matt continued, "I was especially intrigued by the problem you gave them for next Tuesday. I have to admit, I wouldn't want to have to choose whether to rescue the *Mona Lisa* or an old, sick man from a burning building. How would you solve the dilemma?"

"For a lot of years I saved the painting."

"And now?"

She shrugged. "I grew up. I've seen more of life's ups and downs." She smiled as she admitted, "And I've lost my fondness for the *Mona Lisa.* How about you? Would you save the old man or the painting?"

"You gave the class until Tuesday to think about it. Don't I get the same consideration?"

"All right. But I'll be looking forward to hearing what you have to say." Jenny checked her watch. "It's nearly lunchtime. Are you hungry?"

"A little. You must have worked up quite an appetite with all that pacing in class."

"I did."

"Come on. I know a good place to get a pastrami sandwich."

Matt gathered up the rope between them as though he were a cowboy collecting his lariat. By tacit agreement he'd become the keeper of the extra length of rope when they traveled from one place to another. Still, they had to leave a foot or so of slack between them so they wouldn't accidentally run into each other when they walked, and with the crowds on the street, they occasionally had to stop and wait for someone coming from the other direction to realize they were tied together. Despite that problem, so far they'd remained fairly inconspicuous, which just proved you had to do something pretty spectacular to get noticed in New York.

Matt took her to a small Jewish deli, where the pastrami was as good as he'd promised. When they'd nearly finished eating, Jenny reached for the check, only to have Matt intercept it. She bristled until he said, "Your half of the tab is $15.87." He stared at her for another moment, a smile lurking at the corners of his mouth. "Does that sound satisfactory to you, *Ms.* Smith?"

Jenny laughed and handed him her credit card. "Touché! Although, by rights, I ought to pay the whole bill, since you wouldn't be here right now, if it weren't for my project."

Matt loved the sound of her laughter. "I'd have to eat, even if I were still working full-time," he said as he added cash to cover his half of the check and the tip. "I feel as though I'm playing hooky from school."

And playing—with her—was exactly what he had in mind. He wanted to put his mouth on her skin so badly he could almost taste it already. He was looking forward to the days ahead, especially the challenge of getting her into his bed. "By the way," he said, "you have a beautiful smile."

Her smile instantly disappeared. "Why would you say something like that?"

"I don't know what you mean."

"My looks are irrelevant."

"So you don't want to hear that I've been thinking about what it might be like to kiss that mole beside your mouth? Or how much I'd like to—"

"No! I don't want to be seen as an attractive female. At least not for the next thirty days."

"You're removing sex entirely from the equation? That hardly seems realistic, when I'm male and you're female."

"We're also *people*. Can't you just think of me as one of the guys?"

Jenny felt her body responding as Matt's gray eyes caressed her face, moved to her throat, and then downward all the way to her toes. She crossed her arms over her chest to hide her physical response to his provocative behavior, huffed out a breath, and said, "That's enough. Stop."

He raised his gaze to her face again, but his look was no less intimate.

Jenny tilted her head in exasperation and stared him down.

Finally, he shrugged and said, "I'll do my best to avoid looking at you as a woman, but it won't be easy." He shoved aside his plate and settled his elbows on the table. "What do you have planned for us the rest of the day?"

"I don't really have anything planned," Jenny admitted. "I thought we'd play things by ear. You know, just feel things out."

"It's *not* feeling that's going to be the problem," Matt countered with a wry smile. When Jenny wrinkled her nose, he said, "I haven't seen a movie in the afternoon in years. How does that sound to you?"

"Fine. Let's go see that comedy with—"

"Uh-uh. I'm in the mood for some action and adventure. How about that new cop—"

"Blood and gore? No way," Jenny protested.

"What about that sci-fi—"

"I don't like sci-fi. I vote for a romance. There's a new French film—"

"You're not actually going to suggest that the two of us sit in a dark theatre and watch some man and woman breathing heavily on each other all afternoon."

Jenny raised a brow.

Matt exhaled noisily. "I see you have exactly that in mind. Does that seem wise to you? I mean, under the circumstances?"

"It's a good test of my theory," Jenny said. "After all, I want to prove that a man and woman can be more to each other than prospective sexual partners. Just because we watch a romance on the screen doesn't mean we have to project ourselves into the same situation."

"It sounds to me like a severe test of my willpower."

"Come on. You don't really believe either one of us is going to fall all over the other, just because we watch some man and woman making love in a movie, do you?"

"Yes, I do," he shot back. "I think you're making a big mistake. But this is your project. If a sexy French movie is all we can agree on, it's better than nothing. Lead the way."

Matt was right, Jenny conceded fifteen minutes into the film, when the first bare flesh appeared on the screen. The movie was a mistake. They'd separated themselves by a single seat, so they wouldn't accidentally brush elbows or knees in the darkness of the theatre. But Jenny was one of those people who used the movies the way they were intended. She completely lost herself in the fantasy presented on the big screen. So when the dark-haired, blue-eyed Frenchman caressed the female lead, Jenny felt his gentle, callused fingertips on her skin. When his lips hovered over the woman's, Jenny felt the tightening deep within her that signaled the beginning of desire. Her tongue came out to moisten her lips in unconscious preparation for the coming kiss.

When Matt saw Jenny lick her lips, he was ready to get up and walk out. She was crazy if she thought a movie like this would be easy for either of them to sit through. But he'd be damned if he'd give her the satisfaction of seeing him discomfited by the sex on the screen. "Are you all right?" he whispered.

Jenny saw Matt was shifting in his seat. It seemed he wasn't enjoying this sexual torment any more than she was. "I'm fine," she whispered back.

Jenny's attention turned back to the screen. It wasn't just a man and a woman up there. It was Matt and Jenny. She closed her eyes as her blood began to rush in her veins. Her breathing became labored, as though she were one of the slick bodies writhing in pleasure on silk sheets.

Good grief, Jenny! What's wrong with you? Matt is a person, not a sexual object. How could you be using him this way? He'd be furious if he knew what you were thinking.

No he wouldn't. He'd be pleased.

So you say.

He'd say a man and a woman were created to be together like this, so why fight it?

Who says I'm fighting it?

Then open your eyes.

I can't.

Do you believe in this project or not?

Jenny opened her eyes. The woman's face filled the screen, and Jenny knew from her beatific expression that she was in the throes of passion. When the man's face came on the screen, Jenny saw Matt's face. Saw the perspiration dotting *his* upper lip, saw the agonized lines of pleasure on *his* brow, saw the hooded lids fall sensually over *his* dilated eyes.

Oh, Lord. It was happening again.

Jenny jumped up and yanked on the rope. "Let's go!"

Matt remained seated, his popcorn in his lap, in no condition to leave the concealing darkness of the theater . "What's the matter?" he whispered. "Don't you like the movie?"

"Down in front!" an angry voice shouted.

Jenny's knees were shaking so badly, it didn't take much effort for her to drop back into her seat. Once there, she slumped down as far as she could get. How humiliating! She closed her eyes, then crossed her arms and legs, waiting for the movie to be over. Even though she couldn't see, she could still hear the sighs, the whispered words of love.

Finally, she couldn't stand the agony one moment longer. She leaned across the empty chair and snapped at Matt, "We have to leave. Now!"

With her nostrils flared and her eyes liquid in the light from the screen, Matt had no trouble at all picturing Jenny with her blond hair spread across a pillow, her chest heaving under him. He rose and pulled her after him out of the theater and onto the street. The two of them blinked owlishly and staggered a little, waiting for their eyes to make the transition from darkness to bright sunlight.

"Where to now, *Ms.* Smith?" Matt asked, with what seemed to her a pretty smug smile on his face.

"I was wrong to suggest that film."

"No kidding."

Jenny realized Matt's eyes were lambent, his cheeks flushed, and a hard ridge had appeared beneath the zipper in his jeans. She took a deep, cleansing breath. Matt hadn't survived the influence of the film any better than she had. The sooner they left the theater behind, the better. "I know a place where we can make a quick stop for coffee and buy a coffeemaker. Then I'd like to go home because I need . . . I want . . ."

"Want what?"

"Don't rush me. I'm thinking."

Jenny realized that what she really wanted was a little time alone to compose herself. She looked at the silky white cord that hung slack between them and sighed. She wasn't going to get her wish. Wherever she went, Matt would have to follow.

She glanced at her watch. Not even eight hours together, and she was already fantasizing about being in bed with the man. She was distressed by her reaction, because she'd honestly believed the premise she'd set out to prove. The sexes *could* appreciate one another on more than one level. Yes, they were different; she wasn't trying to deny that. But they each had something valuable to offer the other. She just couldn't understand what it was about Matt Benson that made her so vulnerable to him as a man.

"What have you decided?" Matt asked.

Nature gave Jenny some help. There was only one bathroom she knew with a notch in the door to accommodate the rope between them. "Let's get your coffee stuff and go home."

CHAPTER SIX

When they arrived at her apartment, Jenny did everything she could think of to avoid the inevitable trip to the bathroom. Finally, she could wait no longer. She'd known it would be embarrassing not to have any privacy; she just hadn't known how embarrassing. It reminded her of the day after her wedding, when she'd seen her family for the first time. They'd known what she'd been doing with Sam all night. It showed in the rosy blush on her face and in the well-kissed look of her mouth. When she came out of the bathroom in a few minutes she expected to be met by that same knowing look from Matt.

Jenny was relieved, when she opened the bathroom again, to find him lying on the bed closest to the bathroom with his eyes closed. If she hadn't known better, she would have said he was asleep. But, of course, he wasn't.

"Which bed is yours?" he asked without opening his eyes.

"I'll take the other one, since you seem to have claimed that one."

He opened his eyes and turned lazily onto his side, resting his head on his hand. "I'll be glad to move, if you'd rather I use the other bed. I only thought that, since you'll probably be using the facilities more than I will, this would be more convenient for both of us."

"That's a rather sexist assumption," Jenny said, annoyed because it was also true. When he started to move to the other bed, she said, "Never mind. Stay where you are. I usually sleep in the bed closest to the living room."

Matt eyed Jenny speculatively. She was standing with her chin thrust mulishly forward, suggesting that, even though she'd just apologized, she didn't like the position he'd put her in. Well, that went double for him. "Are you going to analyze everything I say over the next thirty days for its sexist connotation?"

"I told you I'm sorry," she said, settling cross-legged on the other bed. "Are you sure you're not being deliberately provocative?"

Matt smiled wryly. "Honey, I'm just being myself, but it doesn't seem to take much—"

Jenny stopped him right there. "I've asked you not to call me *honey*."

Matt lay back on the bed and laughed.

"I don't know what you find so funny."

"You," he said between chuckles.

Jenny shook her head in exasperation. "You're the one who's impossible!"

"No, sweetheart, I'm just a man."

Jenny glared. *Sweetheart* wasn't much of an improvement over *honey,* and that *man* had to know it.

"Truce?" Matt said, sitting up and holding his open palms out in front of him. "Otherwise, it's going to be a long thirty days."

"All right," Jenny reluctantly agreed. "Truce."

"How about fixing us some supper? I'm hungry."

"You know where the kitchen is."

"I'm happy to wait until you make something. Then I'll have a little of whatever you're having."

Jenny did a slow burn. "Are you sure you'd be willing to eat a meal prepared by li'l ole me, darlin'?"

Matt grinned. "You cook it. I'll eat it."

Jenny picked up the phone and called her favorite Chinese takeout. "We can pick it up in a few minutes. Your half comes to $12.15."

Matt pulled out his wallet and threw a five and a ten at her. "By the time you get the table set, the food will be here."

Jenny narrowed her eyes. *"We'll* have the table set," she corrected. "Whither one goest, the other will go," she said, heading for the kitchen.

Matt laughed as her tug on the rope forced him off the bed.

She'd just reached the living room when her home phone rang. She picked up the extension on the end table beside the couch and said, "Hello." She listened for a moment before she held out the phone to Matt. "It's for you. A woman."

"That'll be Rachel Stephens. I gave her your number." Matt plopped down on the couch, and Jenny headed to the nearby kitchen to set the table.

"Hello, Rachel. Are we still on for tomorrow? Right. I'll pick you up at—" Matt held his hand over the phone and asked Jenny, "Can you be ready to go out to dinner tomorrow at seven-thirty?"

"We're going to dinner?"

"I have a date with Rachel, and, as I recall, you said this project wasn't going to interfere with my personal plans. Can you be ready at seven-thirty?"

"I guess so. Sure."

"You there, Rachel? How about if I meet you at the usual place at eight o'clock? Fine. Bye, honey. 'Til tomorrow. Hmm. I can imagine. See you soon."

Matt's voice had become husky during his farewell, and a sensuous smile lit his face in response to whatever it was Rachel had said that he could "imagine." Jenny didn't need much insight to guess what that might be.

Matt hung up the phone, then began dialing again. "I suppose a liberated woman like you doesn't bother with a sexist activity like dating, so I'll make a reservation for three."

"As a matter of fact," Jenny said, "I have a date for tomorrow night myself. We just hadn't made any special plans. We'll be glad to join you and Rachel for dinner."

"Who might the lucky man be?"

Jenny had to think fast. Who could she call on such short notice to be her date? "Why . . . it's . . ." She quickly considered and rejected several men before she said, "Patrick, of course."

Matt frowned. "The photographer?"

"Yes. Patrick the photographer."

"Isn't he a little young for you?"

"How much older than Rachel are you?"

"That's beside the point."

"That's *exactly* the point," Jenny argued. "A man reaches his sexual prime in his teens. A woman reaches hers in her thirties. It makes infinitely more sense for an older woman to date a younger man. They're more sexually compatible."

"You don't say."

Matt's expression made it clear he wasn't willing to concede the point. "It's clear I'm not going to change your mind about this, so why don't we sit down here in the kitchen and—"

Jenny had already headed for her chair when Matt pulled on the rope that tied them together, so she came to a quick halt. "Turn around, Jenny." He tugged on the rope until she turned to face him.

Jenny folded her arms defiantly across her chest. "What do you want, Matt?"

"Are you saying a man, like me, isn't capable of arousing a woman, like you, when he gets past a certain age?"

"Of course I wasn't making such a ridiculous statement," Jenny retorted.

"Then you admit that I'd have no problem arousing you sexually?"

Jenny's eyes widened in disbelief as Matt set down the phone without making his reservation at a restaurant, stood up, and stalked toward her, gathering the slack rope between them as he came.

"Just what do you think—"

"Come here, Jenny," he said, his voice coaxing, as though he were soothing some wild thing he'd lassoed and wanted to hold in his hands.

Jenny was transfixed by the desire in his eyes. He tugged her closer and closer, until there was no more than an inch separating their bodies. She could feel his breath on her face, and they might as well have been touching, since she was aware of his body heat. It frightened her to realize how much she yearned to reach out and touch him. She stiffened her muscles in an attempt to stop their trembling.

"Admit it," he murmured. "You want me."

She stiffened her spine and said in an icy voice, "So what if I do? Believe me, I can resist you. What are you trying to prove by this little demonstration?"

Matt's gaze dropped to the nipples peaking beneath her blouse. "The premise of this art project is as full of holes as a wormy apple, Jenny. The sexes were never meant to be separate. As for being equal—well, I've always applauded the *differences* between a man and a woman."

Matt's attack on her project with another food metaphor set up her hackles. First it was moldy bread. Now it was wormy apples! She was irritated with Matt for taking advantage of the sensual attraction she felt for him and even more irritated with herself, for letting down her guard. She backed a few steps away before she spoke.

"I don't doubt you've relegated the women you've known to certain limited places in your life—the kitchen and the bedroom," she said, her voice dripping with scorn. "The point I want to make with this project is that a woman should be more to a man than a cook and a maid and a good time in bed. If you spend a month with me, you'll see that I have the same hopes and desires, the same frustrations and disappointments, as any man. I'm not just a woman. I'm a person."

Jenny's description of his behavior—which was pretty much on the money—nevertheless left Matt feeling shallow and callous. What did the woman expect from him? The whole project struck him as absurd. A Rembrandt superimposed on a Picasso. Nothing fit together. "I hear what you're saying. It remains to be seen whether your arguments hold up to scrutiny."

Jenny huffed out a frustrated breath. "Are you going to give this project a chance to succeed? Or not?"

"I wasn't aware your success or failure depended on me."

"What I mean is, are you going to sabotage my project by tempting me to touch you the whole time?"

"I'm sorry if it seemed like I was playing games with you. But if you'll remember, I promised not to touch you. I didn't promise not to try to get you to touch me."

When Jenny gasped, he added, "Before you interrupt, hear me out. I've never made any bones about the fact that I don't agree with your point of view. Women and men aren't meant to be separate. They're two parts of a whole. As for being equal, they aren't. It's as simple as that."

"That's it? Are you finished?"

"I'm finished."

Jenny marched up to Matt and would have poked a finger in his chest, if it hadn't meant touching him. She let her voice do the poking instead. "Two parts of a whole? Three-quarters male and one-quarter female, I suppose. I agree with your opinion on the lack of equality between the sexes. There isn't a man alive who can measure up to a woman. Stuff that in your pipe and smoke it, macho man!"

"You're beautiful when you're angry."

Jenny stepped away as though she'd been slapped. "Trite, Mr. Benson."

"True, *Ms*. Smith." He dropped into a chair at the table. "Come on, Jenny. This isn't getting us anywhere. I'm hungry. Let's take this thing one step at a time. You know where I stand, and you know what you can do about it. I've promised I won't touch you. If you can't keep from touching me, well, that's what this whole project is about, isn't it?"

"You've made your point," Jenny said. "There's no need to say another word. Let's go pick up the food. I want to have dinner and turn in early. It's been a long day."

And she had a feeling it was going to be an even longer night.

CHAPTER SEVEN

Jenny didn't ask for help cleaning up the kitchen after dinner, and Matt didn't offer. Actually, she was too caught up in her thoughts to pay much attention to what was happening around her. She hadn't imagined how stressful it was going to be spending every moment in Matt's company. For instance, it would have been wonderful, after their argument, to sulk alone in her bedroom. No such luck. She'd been forced to endure his cheerful company.

Of even more concern at the moment was how she was going to get in touch with Patrick about their supposed date. Of course! Matt was going to have to use the bathroom sometime. When he did, she'd call Patrick on her cell.

"Are you ready for bed?" Matt asked.

"What? Oh, yes. Sure."

"Who's first in the bathroom tonight?"

There it was again, Jenny thought, that enforced

discussion of intimate subjects by two people who were strangers. "You can go first." That would give her a chance to make her call.

Matt led the way to the bedroom. He had his shirt off and was unbuckling his belt when he heard Jenny's hesitant cough.

"Umm. Could you do that in the bathroom?"

Matt looked up to find Jenny's gaze locked on the dark curls that covered his chest. "No problem." At least, there wouldn't be, if he got into the bathroom before his body revealed what having her look at him with admiration was doing to him.

Jenny breathed a sigh of relief as the bathroom door closed behind Matt. In another minute, she would've completely embarrassed herself, the way she was ogling his six-pack. She shook her head to clear it of any lingering effects of Matt's physique and punched out Patrick's number.

The call went straight to voice mail.

She heard the shower go on and imagined Matt stripped down. She dialed Patrick again and breathed easier when the phone started ringing.

"Patrick, this is Jenny Smith."

"Hi, Jenny. This is a surprise. What's up?"

"I need a favor."

"Anything for my favorite professor."

"You'd better wait to hear what I want before you agree."

"Shoot."

"I want you to go on a date—for dinner—with me tomorrow night."

There was a stunned silence on the other end of the line.

"Patrick? Are you there?"

"I'm here."

Silence again.

"Patrick, I'll understand if you have something else—"

"No." She heard a quick gulp. "No, I'd enjoy going to dinner. You just surprised me. I didn't think you dated."

"I don't."

"Oh."

Jenny heard the shower being turned off and knew she didn't have much time. "I can't explain right now, Patrick. Please, I just need you to show up here tomorrow night at seven-thirty as though we've had this date for a while. Can you do that for me?"

"Sure. But why—"

The bathroom door started to open.

"Goodbye, Patrick," Jenny whispered as she ended the call.

Steam rolled out as soon as the bathroom door opened, and Jenny was confronted by the sight of Matt with one of her fluffy, sky-blue towels slung low on his hips.

"No ventilation," Matt said. "Figured I'd better open the door."

"I've been meaning to get that fan fixed."

"Maybe I can do it while I'm here."

Jenny wasn't paying much attention to the conversation and heard herself reply, "Sure. Anything you say." He had a lovely navel, and she could hardly take her eyes off the line of dark curls that disappeared under the towel. His hair was wet, and water dripped down the sides of his neck and over his forehead. He yanked another towel off the rack just inside the door and used it to blot the soaked rope around his waist.

"Can you help me with this? Do the back?"

Jenny walked toward him like someone in a trance. She took the towel from him and blotted the rope at his back, careful not to touch his body. She could feel the play of his muscles under the towel and worked quickly to finish up. "If this wet rope gets uncomfortable, you can use the hair dryer to finish drying it."

"It's no bother. Don't worry about it."

She couldn't help swiping up the droplets of water that had caught along the crease in his back. Once she'd started, it was hard to stop. She worked her way all the way up his spine to his shoulders. "There."

"Thanks." He took the towel from her and slung it around his neck, wiping the streaming water off his face, as he carefully squeezed past her and out of the bathroom. "Your turn."

Jenny closed the door after him without quite realizing what she was doing. She turned to lean her back against the wood and looked down at her hands. They were shaking. Her gaze slid to the bathroom floor, and she almost laughed out loud at what she found.

At the top of a small pile of dirty clothes was the first pair of what she suspected would soon be a tidy heap of Matthew Benson's undershorts.

After her shower, Jenny blotted the rope, just as Matt had, and realized he was right. The dampness at her waist was noticeable but not uncomfortable. She wrapped herself in two towels, one above and one below the rope, so she looked like some kind of Polynesian dancer. By the time she opened the bathroom door, Matt was already in bed. He was sitting up reading, the sheet settled at his waist. His broad chest was a mass of dark curls, and she realized she was itching to run her fingers through them. What had she been thinking when she'd conceived this project? Certainly not about this sensual torture.

"Aren't you going to wear pajamas?" she asked.

"Didn't bring any."

"Oh." She gave him a sidelong look. Surely he was wearing *something* under that sheet.

"How about you? Going to sleep in those towels?"

"I usually sleep in a T-shirt. I didn't have one with me in the bathroom."

"Go ahead and put one on. I won't look," he said with a grin.

Jenny figured she could trust Matt about as far as she could throw him. However, she was prepared for just this situation. She took her T-shirt and some clean bikini underwear behind a screen she'd put in a corner of the bedroom.

From the corner of his eye, Matt saw both towels come to rest on top of the screen. She would be naked now. He liked the way her blond hair brushed her shoulders right out of the shower. She should let it hang free all the time, instead of keeping it tied up on her head the way she did. He imagined grabbing a handful of the silky stuff and angling her head back for his kiss. He raised his knees under the sheet to hide the evidence of his arousal. Damn. What had he gotten himself into? This was agony.

Jenny felt self-conscious when she came out from behind the screen. She was fully dressed, but from the look Matt was giving her, she might as well have been naked.

Abruptly Matt threw his book down on the table between the two beds and turned onto his side, facing away from her.

"Are you going to sleep already?" Jenny asked. It was barely ten-thirty.

"I usually get up early." He made a disgruntled sound in his throat. "When are you going to turn out the light?"

"Soon," Jenny promised. "I want to read a little. It helps me to wind down."

She was still reading twenty minutes later when Matt startled her by sitting up.

"What's the matter?" she asked.

"I can't sleep with that light on. You're going to have to turn it off."

Jenny stared at his broad chest, at his tousled hair, at his lazy bedroom eyes. "I usually read until midnight."

"Not for the next thirty days, you don't."

Jenny didn't want to argue. If she argued with Matt, he might stand up, and . . . What if he wasn't wearing anything under that sheet? "All right. Turn over and go back to sleep. As soon as I finish this chapter—"

"Now."

When he reached for the sheet that covered him, Jenny acknowledged that she had a tiger by the tail. They could argue this out in the light of day. She marked her place, set the book calmly on the nightstand, and reached over to turn out the light, plunging the room into darkness. She heard the sheets rustle, as he settled back in bed. As quietly as she could, she settled herself as well.

"Jenny . . ."

"Yes?"

"You're a work of art in that T-shirt."

"Trite, Mr. Benson."

"True, *Ms.* Smith."

It took all Jenny's willpower to turn away from him.

He was a man who made her feel like a woman. How was she going to last thirty days without touching him?

CHAPTER EIGHT

When Jenny had come up with the idea of tying two people together with a rope, she hadn't considered sleeping patterns. Who would have imagined that Matt would be such a restless sleeper?

It wouldn't have been so bad that he tossed and turned in his sleep, except he kept turning in the same direction, gradually winding the rope around his waist. By the middle of the night, the rope between them had been pulled taut enough that Matt's next turn jerked Jenny out of bed. She landed on the floor with a cry, startling Matt awake.

"What the hell?"

"For heaven's sake," Jenny said when she finally had the light on. "Look what you've done." The rope tangled around Matt's waist bore testimony to what had happened.

When Matt stood to untangle the rope, Jenny gasped and focused her gaze on her feet. He hadn't been naked, but that single glimpse had given her a pretty good impression of every wonderful masculine thing his navy briefs did little to conceal.

He swore under his breath as he turned to untangle himself. Then he looked at her with concern and asked, "Are you all right? You're not hurt?"

"I'm fine," Jenny had said, suddenly breathless. She slid back into bed and turned away from Matt. "Get the light, will you?"

It seemed she'd barely gotten back to sleep when she felt another tug at her waist. Still half asleep, she reached down to see what was causing the problem. She'd forgotten completely about the rope. Something was jerking on it.

Jenny turned over and leaned up on one elbow. The clock showed 5:00 a.m. Matt was on the floor at the foot of his bed, and he was doing sit-ups. She watched his rippling muscles in awe as he changed from sit-ups to push-ups. "What are you doing awake at this hour of the morning?" she croaked.

"I always exercise in the morning. Keeps me in shape."

"Oh, my God," she moaned. Jenny noticed he wasn't even breathing hard, although a fine sheen of perspiration coated his well-conditioned body. From the waist down he was hidden from her by his bed. Thank goodness. She slid back down and closed her eyes, determined to ignore him.

Jenny had barely gotten back to sleep, when she heard a husky whisper in her ear.

"Do you suppose you could slip into my bed so I could take a shower?"

Jenny growled. "Anything. Just let me sleep. Pleeeease." She barely opened her eyes, just groped her way to the other bed. She hadn't been in Matt's bed for more than a minute when she realized she could smell him on the bedclothes. She sniffed at the feather pillow she held snuggled in her arms. It was almost as though she held *him* in her arms. Except the pillow was soft, and she imagined Matt's body would be hard. She sniffed again, then jerked her head upright as she realized what she was doing.

It was 5:45 a.m., and Jenny was suddenly wide awake. Well, she thought wryly, at least she was no longer *sleeping* in Matt's bed. She could hear him singing in the shower—a popular Broadway tune—and he wasn't a half-bad baritone. How was she going to survive the next twenty-nine days of this insanity?

By 6:00 a.m. Matt was out of the shower. He wanted her to make him some coffee. Jenny wanted to sleep.

"Come on, Jenny. You went to bed half an hour earlier than usual last night. A cup of coffee will get you going."

Jenny opened one bleary eye and announced, "If you'll recall, I don't drink coffee."

"Then you can make yourself some tea." Matt started pulling the sheet down, and Jenny grabbed at it.

"All right," she mumbled. "Just let me go to the bathroom, if you don't mind."

"I don't mind at all." He gestured her toward the bathroom door.

Matt grinned and Jenny realized what he was gawking at. The T-shirt had ridden up under the sheets exposing her bikini panties. She gasped and bolted out of bed as though she'd been stung.

His laughter followed her into the bathroom.

Jenny took her time washing her face, brushing her teeth, and slipping in her contact lenses, then padded after Matt into the kitchen. "This is an inhuman time to be awake," she grumbled.

"You miss the best part of the day, if you're not up to see the sunrise."

"Thanks, but no thanks."

Matt had put some coffee on to perk in the coffeemaker and had turned the burner on under the kettle of water Jenny had left there the previous night. "Don't say I never did you any favors. Now, what are you going to make us for breakfast?"

"I don't want any breakfast. I want to go back to bed."

"Pancakes sound good to me. Here, I'll help. I'll get the mix down from the cupboard for you."

She had to admit the pancakes she made tasted good. But she spent most of breakfast blinking her right eye, trying to focus it. Even her *eyes* knew it wasn't time to get up yet. Her right contact lens was so blurry, she was having trouble seeing, and she was seriously considering taking the thing out and putting on her glasses. She was vain enough to keep blinking, though, hoping the lens would clear.

She slept unashamedly with her head on her arms while Matt put the dishes in the dishwasher and had a second cup of coffee. When she felt the tug at her waist, she rose like a zombie and followed him back into the bedroom. She lay down on Matt's bed again while he headed into the bathroom.

"Where is the damn thing?"

At Matt's furious exclamation, Jenny sat up in bed and asked, "Where's what?"

Matt pulled the bathroom door open and said, "I've lost one of my contact lenses. I thought I put them both in the case last night, but I must have dropped one."

Jenny took turns with Matt searching the bathroom floor, but without any luck.

"I don't have an extra set of lenses. We're going to have to go by my optometrist's office before tonight."

To Jenny's way of thinking, the tortoise-shell glasses he'd put on did nothing to make him look any less attractive. But Matt remained adamant about needing a new lens before his date with Rachel.

"Girls never make passes at guys who wear glasses, huh?" she teased.

Matt wasn't amused.

He still needed to shave, she needed to put on her makeup, and there was only one bathroom. They flipped a coin to see who would go first. It didn't seem to help Matt's temper when he lost.

"I'll be out as quickly as I can," Jenny said.

She kept winking and blinking the whole time she was putting on her makeup, but her right contact didn't get any clearer. With a sigh, she took it out and opened the right side of her lens case to put it away.

But there was already a contact lens in the right side of her case.

Jenny opened the bathroom door. "Matt?"

"What?" he asked from his sitting position at the head of the bed.

"I . . . uh . . . found your contact lens."

He was standing beside her an instant later. "Where was it?"

"In my eye."

"What?"

"I must not have been paying attention when I put my lenses in this morning. It seems I put in my left lens and your right one. Both cases were on the sink and . . ."

Jenny shrugged apologetically.

Matt threw back his head and laughed. "I can't believe it! You never noticed the difference?"

"It looks just like mine," Jenny protested. "And it didn't feel uncomfortable. It just looked a little blurry."

"I guess your eyesight is worse than mine," Matt said with a grin.

"I guess so." Jenny couldn't help smiling back at him. He was awfully attractive when he smiled.

"Hurry up and finish," Matt said. "I've got thirty minutes of walking to do before I get started today."

Jenny gaped. "Say that again."

"What?"

"That part about the thirty minutes of walking."

Matt looked sheepish as he admitted, "I usually run in the mornings, as well as do exercises. I realized that wouldn't be possible this month, so I thought I'd compromise with a brisk walk."

"I do enough walking in New York without volunteering to do more."

"Come on, Jenny," Matt said. "It'll be good for you. Get your heart pumping."

Matt was close enough that Jenny's heart was doing a fine job of pumping without the need for a thirty-minute walk.

"Please, Jenny?"

He was like a little boy asking for the other half of her popsicle. Jenny had always been a sucker for sad eyes and a pout. "All right. But I expect you to keep your pace matched to mine."

"Agreed. If we walk for half an hour, we'll be just in time to meet Stan Zimmerman at his gallery when it opens."

Jenny stood up in surprise. "But I have to work this morning. I thought you'd be coming with me."

"You said you only taught Tuesdays and Thursdays."

"I do. But I also told you I have another source of income. I spend the rest of the week at my studio," Jenny explained.

"What studio?"

"It's a loft over a boutique in Soho. I work there with a friend of mine."

"What do you do? I thought your specialty was performance art."

"It is, but I make my living creating wearable art for the boutique downstairs from the studio."

"This I've got to see."

Jenny sat down cross-legged on Matt's bed while he headed into the bathroom. It was an intimate thing, she realized, to watch a man shave. She ignored the tensing in the pit of her stomach, as he slathered lather over his cheeks, chin, and throat.

He took the first swipe with his razor, and while he was rinsing it under running water said, "I've heard about wearable art, but I haven't paid much attention to it. Do you enjoy your work?"

"I love it. I use a mixture of unlikely fabrics, add leather, lace, baubles, a variety of trims—everything from dried pasta to drapery cord—and create something to wear that's unique enough to be called art. I also do accessories—hats, purses, shoes, and jewelry."

"Women pay good money for that sort of thing?"

Jenny shrugged to disguise her shiver, as Matt stroked the razor from his Adam's apple up to his chin. "The few who can afford it."

He shot her an astonished look. "What you make is

that expensive?"

"They're buying a piece of art, a piece of an artist's heart and soul. It doesn't come cheap." Jenny swallowed as Matt finished shaving and rinsed off the last of the lather, leaving the angled planes of his face bare to her gaze. She'd wondered how he shaved those long grooves on either side of his mouth. She almost giggled out loud as she thought, *Very carefully!*

Matt glanced sideways at Jenny. Her eyes hadn't left him the whole time he'd been shaving. Hell, he'd almost nicked himself twice trying to get the whole business over with before his trembling hand cut his throat. How could a woman—especially this woman—affect him so strongly? He shook off the lingering effects of having her eyes focused on him and said, "The way you've explained it, a simple skirt and blouse can be elevated to something like a Botticelli."

"Wearable art doesn't have to rival Botticelli to be enjoyed," Jenny argued. She glanced out the bathroom door and caught a glimpse of the clock beside the bed. "I can't believe this. It's only 8:00 a.m.!"

"How did you get so caught up in what time it is?"

"I'm not—"

"You looked at your watch twelve times last night."

When she opened her mouth to protest he said, "I counted. And God knows how many times you've checked the time this morning."

"Thanks to you, I certainly got an early start," Jenny shot back. "I like to know what time it is. What's wrong with that?"

"Nothing, I suppose. But it makes you different from a lot of other artists I know."

"How so?"

"You can't be unfettered and independent, spontaneous, if you will, when you're watching a clock. Being time-bound takes away the freedom to do things whenever you feel like it."

Jenny shook her head in disbelief. "How do you manage to get where you need to be on time?"

"Sometimes I'm late," Matt admitted. "But if I am, it's because I haven't let a clock stop me when I was having a good time doing something else."

"That sounds more like irresponsibility than freedom," Jenny countered.

"Want to try it for a day—as an experiment, like this project?"

Jenny's eyes narrowed suspiciously. "What would I have to do?"

"First, take off your watch."

After a moment of thought, she complied.

"Now, don't think about what time it is for the rest of the day."

Jenny's lips pursed while she waged an inner battle. "To be honest, I'm not sure I can do that."

"I didn't think I could spend thirty days tied to a beautiful woman without touching her, but I'm managing. Where's your sense of adventure?"

Jenny didn't know whether to be flattered that he thought she was beautiful or furious that he'd agreed to be her partner when he had reservations. His challenge spurred her to say, "All right. You're on. Since you're aiming to break one of my habits, it seems only fair for me to take a shot at breaking one of yours."

Matt had a sinking feeling he knew what was coming. She didn't disappoint him.

"If I manage to make it through the day without asking

about the time, you have to go a day without cigarettes."

"And if you don't make it?"

"Then I'll take down my No Smoking sign and bring in an ashtray so you can have your evening cigarette in bed."

That sounded great to Matt, and he was pretty sure Jenny wouldn't last long without needing to know the time.

"What do I get if I win?" she asked.

"What did you have in mind?"

"I get to read till midnight."

"Works for me. Now, are you ready for that walk?"

Jenny fought the urge to look at her watch. "Whenever you are. Where are we going after our walk? I do have to work, Matt. It's how I pay the rent."

"How about a compromise?" he suggested. "Let me spend an hour or so checking out this artist's work, and then I'll come with you to your studio. I can write up my reactions while you're working. How does that sound?"

"Fine, except how will I know when your hour is up?"

Matt laughed. "You can count the seconds under your breath, if it'll make you feel better."

"I just might," Jenny muttered. "Are you ready to go?"

"I need to put in my newfound lens."

Jenny fought a blush of embarrassment. "No problem. I'll wait." She smiled and added, "For however long it takes."

CHAPTER NINE

When they walked out the front door of her apartment, Jenny unconsciously looked at her wrist to see what time it was.

Matt smirked.

"We'd better get moving," she said. "We'll be—" Jenny bit her tongue to keep from making a reference to how late they were going to be, if they didn't hurry.

There was one good thing about Matt's challenge. Jenny was so busy worrying about what time it was that she completely forgot about the fact that they were tied together. The whole time they walked, her mind was concentrated on whether they'd be late for Matt's appointment. Not that she cared, of course. If he wanted to spend his whole life missing the party, who was she to suggest he do otherwise?

Jenny couldn't help wondering, though, what it would be like to live with someone who was so cavalier about time. She'd learned her lesson the hard way. Life was intended to be lived every minute. You never knew when the fates were going to step in and steal it away. Jenny kept track of time because she knew it was not an unlimited commodity. Without her watch, she felt reckless, as though she were daring the powers that be to rob her while she wasn't paying attention.

"You're quiet," Matt said when they were nearly at their destination.

"I was thinking."

"Mmm?"

Jenny eyed Matt, wondering how to explain her obsession with the clock.

Before she could come up with anything he said, "Here we are."

The Soho gallery was no different than a dozen others Jenny had visited. It consisted of a rectangular room with a high ceiling, neutral-colored walls, track lighting, and polished wooden floors, with a few paintings and sculptures tastefully hung or situated at precise intervals.

The gallery owner also reminded Jenny of a dozen others she'd met. He took one look at her and saw a woman, not an artist. It wasn't the first time it had happened, and it wouldn't be the last. She worked to keep her expression neutral and non-judgmental.

The two men greeted one another, shook hands cordially, and then Matt turned to introduce Jenny.

"Jenny, I want you to meet Stan Zimmerman. He owns this gallery. Stan, this is Jenny Smith."

Stan extended his hand to Jenny, and when she reached out to take it, covered it with his own. He used that grip to pull Jenny closer, invading her space until they were uncomfortably close. "Jenny. How lovely you are. Why haven't we met?"

"I've never been here before," Jenny said with a bland smile.

Matt had seen lines delivered more smoothly, but it wasn't Stan's line that bothered him. It was the fact that it had been delivered to Jenny. Did Stan think he'd brought Jenny here just so Stan could make a move on her? He'd soon disabuse him of that notion.To his surprise, Matt found himself wanting to identify Jenny as something more than an attractive female to be leered at; she was someone worth knowing for her own sake. "Jenny's an artist," he said.

"Oh, really?" Stan replied dismissively. He started to lead Jenny away from Matt, saying, "Well, while you're busy out here, I have some paintings in the back that Jenny might enjoy seeing."

On her next step, the rope that bound Jenny to Matt pulled her up short. "Excuse me," she said.

Stan turned, a concerned frown marring his forehead while he tried to figure out what had happened.

"Jenny's staying with me," Matt said.

"Why? There's no reason why she can't—"

Matt held up the rope that bound them and pulled up the extra line until Jenny was standing beside him again. "Sorry, old man. Jenny and I have tied the knot."

"Yes. Well." Stan was clearly flustered and not a little confused. "I didn't know. . . I hadn't heard . . . I'll leave the two of you alone, then. Call me if you need me."

Matt didn't wait for Stan to disappear from the room before he began to chuckle.

"I suppose you thought that little scene was funny," Jenny said.

"Did you see the look on his face?"

"I saw the look on yours."

Matt lifted a questioning brow. "Which was?"

"One male animal challenging another—who'd invaded his territory," Jenny replied tartly.

Matt pulled Jenny a little closer, so there was no more than an inch between them. "You bet. No man's ever stolen my woman and gotten away with it."

The rumbling voice in her ear left Jenny weak-kneed, so she was a little late in protesting Matt's possessiveness. "Of all the idiotic—"

He stepped back abruptly. "Of course, I have no claim on you. But Stan's behavior proves my point."

"Which is?"

"Women are women. Men are men."

"Aaaargh!"

"I'd better get busy." Matt turned and began an intense study of the several paintings Stan had asked him to come there to see.

While Matt examined the artwork, Jenny searched surreptitiously for a clock. She was frustrated beyond belief when there was none to be found. She moved to the end of her tether, hoping that the farther away from Matt she was, the easier it would be to think. It was clear that the past twenty-four hours hadn't moved him off ground zero. Hadn't he recognized the discrimination in Stan's attentions to her? How would he like to be treated strictly as a sexual object? One of the reasons so few women artists got shown in galleries was because they first had to get past the Stan Zimmermans of the world.

Jenny had no idea how much time had passed, but she noticed that Matt had stepped away from the paintings and was now viewing them as a whole, rather than individually.

"What do you think?" Jenny asked.

"They're a perfect example of what happens when an untrained individual tries to create art."

"Then you don't like them."

"I didn't say that. In fact, if I were only looking at this painting—" Matt pointed to a large canvas of a woman seated at a dressing table. "I'd say the artist shows promise."

"Then what did you mean—"

"This particular painting appeals to me. But the rest of these . . ." Matt gestured to the other canvases displayed for his perusal. "Prove that this painting was a fluke, a stroke of luck. No, this lady should have—"

"These paintings were done by a female artist?" Jenny interjected.

"Can't you tell?"

"No. Can you?"

"Of course."

Jenny stared at Matt in awe. "You're either lying or kidding. I can't decide which."

Matt laughed. "In this case it was easy. Artists are like writers. They paint what they know, what they feel. See this background? A woman's vanity, all these knickknacks? That's a woman's subject matter."

"Of all the sexist things I've ever heard you say, I think that's the worst," Jenny said. "I suppose if the painting had depicted race cars, you'd have said it was done by a man."

"It probably would be."

Jenny turned away from Matt and spied a piece of aluminum abstract art. She pointed and said, "All right, smarty-pants. Was that piece created by a male or a female artist?"

"Male. Those two lumps are obviously breasts, and

those two long skinny rods are legs. I'd bet money that piece is a labor of love created by a man."

Jenny stared in amazement at the twisted aluminum. In the first place, the fact that Matt could see a woman in the thing was phenomenal. In the second place, she knew at least two women who spent hours drawing female figures. In the third place . . . he had to be bluffing.

Jenny snickered. "All right, hotshot. Let's get Stan in here to give us the names of these artists."

Jenny spent the whole trip from the Soho gallery to her loft workshop muttering to herself. The woman before the vanity had been painted by a woman. The twisted aluminum sculpture had been created by a man. How had Matt known? Jenny found the experience disconcerting. It seemed Matt was doing a better job of convincing her of the differences between the sexes than she was of convincing him that the sexes were equal.

Jenny was eager to reach her workshop. She hadn't realized precisely why until she saw the clock across from her worktable. She would be able to sneak a peek at the time without having to ask about it.

Matt was on the lookout for a clock, and sure enough he saw it. He stepped ahead of Jenny and turned the clock face toward the wall.

"Why did you do that?" she demanded, hands on hips.

"Wouldn't want you to be tempted to cheat," he said with a grin.

Jenny glowered. But not for long. Her partner wasn't someone who could be ignored, and he promptly introduced himself to Matt, extending a large hand as he did so.

"I'm Russell French."

The man in front of him didn't fit Matt's image of the

typical male fashion designer—even if what he designed was wearable art. He was the size of a linebacker for the New York Jets, with a grip to match. On the other hand, the smile on his face was openly friendly, disarming, even charming.

"Not what you expected?" Russell asked.

Matt was startled that Russell not only recognized his surprise but acknowledged it. He smiled ruefully. "I have to admit I expected someone a little less . . ."

"Large?" Russell said with a smile that acknowledged his enormous height and breadth.

Here was another man in Jenny's life that Matt found hard not to like. He wondered if their business relationship had ever extended into the bedroom, but there was nothing in the easy camaraderie between them to give him an answer one way or the other.

"Russell and I have been working together for four years," Jenny said. "We know each other well enough to survive each other's moods."

The look that passed between Jenny and her partner was comfortable, almost intimate. If they hadn't been lovers, they nonetheless possessed a closeness Matt envied.

"You're late," Russell said to Jenny.

Even though there was no censure in Russell's voice, Matt said promptly, "I'm responsible for that. I had to go by a gallery this morning to view some artwork."

"I just placed you. You're the critic for *Artist's World,* aren't you?" All the pleasantness had gone out of Russell's voice. "The one who panned Jenny's work."

"I am." Matt noticed that Russell suddenly appeared even larger, something like the effect of ruffled plumage on a riled fighting cock.

"I suppose you didn't agree with my review, either," Matt said, carefully holding his ground in the face of Russell's challenging stance.

"No, I didn't." Russell turned to Jenny and said, "I thought I'd talked you out of using this guy for your next project. What changed your mind?"

"I hoped that if Matt followed me around for thirty days, he'd see what I'm trying to do."

"And you expected him to be open-minded enough to admit that he was wrong?"

"I am that open-minded," Matt said, once more drawing Russell's attention. Matt met the other man's steady gaze until Russell turned his back on him and said to Jenny, "We have an entire outfit to finish this afternoon, complete with purse, hat, and shoes."

Jenny was already rolling up her sleeves. "What ti—" Jenny cut herself off just as she was about to ask the time and shot a quick look at Matt. Fortunately, he wasn't paying attention, apparently distracted by the huge amounts of paraphernalia they used to create their wearable art.

"Let's do it," Jenny said.

It was amazing how fast the afternoon passed. Even without her watch, Jenny could tell from the lengthening shadows through the row of windows that lined one wall of the loft that it was getting late. An even better indication of the passing time was the fatigue she felt. Even though she hadn't mentioned the ache in her shoulders, Russell came up behind her and began to massage her aching muscles. Jenny groaned with pleasure.

Matt watched the interplay between Russell and Jenny with consternation. Russell's touch remained merely comforting, the touch of a friend. Matt knew that if he'd been the one massaging Jenny's shoulders, it wouldn't have been long before his hands slipped around to cup her breasts. Which merely confirmed that he thought of Jenny as a woman, rather than merely as a person. Russell treated her as someone special, but not as a sexual someone.

To the best of his knowledge, Matt had never had a woman friend who remained a friend. Somehow the relationship always seemed to progress beyond that, and they became lovers. He could see that the friendship between Russell and Jenny was deep and caring, and that it brought a great deal of satisfaction to both of them. It gave him food for thought. Perhaps that was what Jenny had meant when she'd argued that she was a person as well as a woman.

Jenny rolled her head slowly, enjoying Russell's caring touch. "I'm about ready to call it a day."

"We got everything done but the shoes," Russell said, patting her shoulder. "I can come in tomorrow and take care of them, if you want to get out of here."

"You ready to go, Matt?" Jenny asked.

Matt had finished his review hours ago, but he'd been so fascinated by the creativity he'd witnessed that he hadn't minded the wait. "I guess we'd better get going, if we want to make our reservations at the restaurant tonight."

Jenny groaned. "The last thing I want to do is—"

"You aren't anxious to see Patrick?"

Jenny realized at once the mistake she'd made. Actually, Patrick would be good company. But she would have given a lot to be able to curl up in bed with a good book tonight, instead of heading out on the town. Jenny cursed whatever demons had caused her to lie to Matt about having a date with Patrick. She had no choice now but to make the best of a bad situation. Adding to her dismay was the worry about what she was going to do when the time came to give Patrick a good-night kiss.

CHAPTER TEN

Matt had never seen anything to compare with the dress Jenny had on when she emerged from the bathroom. She'd definitely gone from caterpillar to butterfly. He'd always thought Jenny was beautiful, but he was having trouble taking his eyes off her. The contrasts of texture between lace and leather, and silk and corduroy, the contrasts of color between pink and blue, and red and purple, the multiple layers of cloth in the bodice, the trail of pearls across her shoulder and down to the crevice between her breasts, and the tight, thigh-slit sheath that lovingly enfolded her gorgeous behind, all combined to leave him breathless.

"That outfit is really something," he said. "Is it one of your creations?"

"Yes." Jenny didn't have to ask if Matt liked it. His pleasure at her appearance showed in the warmth of his gray eyes and the curve of his full lips. They'd managed to agree on who would use the bathroom first and where they would dress, so they wouldn't trip over one another, but the occasional tug on the rope when Matt moved kept Jenny constantly aware of the connection between them.

They were both ready before Patrick was scheduled to arrive, so they settled in the living room to wait for him, Jenny in the bamboo chair and Matt on the sofa.

Which gave Jenny time to notice that Matt had donned clothing that emphasized his masculinity. He wore a crisply-starched oxford-cloth shirt that they'd picked up from the laundry on their way back from her workshop, which was open at the throa,t and a pair of dark pleated pants with a leather belt. She imagined herself unbuttoning the shirt. And unbuckling the belt. And unzipping the zipper.

It took her a moment to realize that Matt was watching her as she was inspecting him. His eyes were heavy-lidded, and his body seemed as taut as the rope stretched between them.

"I have to admit I'm surprised we finished dressing on time," Jenny said with a breathless laugh, desperate to diffuse the growing sexual tension. "I could have sworn we wouldn't make it."

Matt rose and began pacing like a lion in a too-small cage. "Goes to show that forgetting about time is one of the best ways of stretching it." He stopped and confronted her. "How did an artist like you get so obsessed with the clock?"

Jenny was saved from answering by a knock on the door. "That'll be Patrick." She wished she'd reminded Patrick not to bring his camera. She was relieved when she opened the door to find him without it. "Patrick. Welcome."

Jenny sensed Matt waiting behind her to see how she greeted Patrick. Figuring some gesture of affection was expected, she rose on tiptoes and kissed her student on the cheek. "I'm glad to see you."

If Patrick was still confused by her abrupt invitation to come to dinner, Jenny saw no signs of it. In fact, he took full advantage of the situation. Before she could step away, he grasped her waist and pulled her close, planting a firm kiss on her lips.

"Hello, Jenny," he said with a pleased grin on his face. "Where are we going tonight?"

Jenny shot a look at Matt and saw a sardonic smile on his face. He extended his hand to Patrick and said, "We meet again. We're headed for Gianni's. It's an Italian place in lower Manhattan. We're meeting a friend of mine there at eight o'clock."

"Then I guess we'd better get going." Patrick placed a proprietary hand under Jenny's elbow. "It's nearly that now."

So much for being on time, Jenny thought, sending a wry glance Matt's way. He merely grinned and shrugged.

"Are we taking a cab or the subway?" Patrick asked.

Matt turned to Jenny, and together they said, "Cab."

Jenny's worst nightmare contained an image of the subway door closing, with her on one side and Matt on the other. She'd made up her mind when she'd decided to do this project that she'd foot the extra expense for a cab when it was necessary to travel farther than walking distance.

Patrick sat between Jenny and Matt in the backseat of the cab, his arm draped over her shoulder. Jenny wished there were some way to get Patrick alone long enough to tell him why she'd asked him out. From his actions, she could see that he considered her invitation sincere, and if current behavior was any guide, she'd have her hands full fending him off before the evening was done.

Rachel Stephens turned out to be a stylishly dressed, long-legged, well-endowed woman with big blue eyes and bright red hair in a shade God could never have fathomed. Jenny guessed she was a good fifteen years younger than Matt.

Rachel gushed. Not that she wasn't sweet, Jenny thought, she just never shut up. How could Matt stand to be around her? Jenny had her answer when they got up to dance after dinner to music provided by an accordion and a violin. Rachel's arms went around Matt's neck, her belly fit into his hips, and Jenny was positive she couldn't have wedged a toothpick between them.

When Matt danced with Rachel, Jenny felt obliged to dance with Patrick. He took his lead from Matt, and before Jenny could protest, she found herself fitted tightly against Patrick's hard body. At least their closeness gave her the chance to explain what was going on.

"Patrick," she whispered.

"Hmm?"

To Jenny's dismay, Patrick was kissing her ear. "Patrick, you have to stop that and listen to me."

"I can hear you just fine." His lips drifted down to her throat.

"Oh, my God," Jenny groaned. "Patrick, listen. About this date—I had to ask you out. I had no choice." Jenny took a deep breath and rattled off, "Matt was going to see Rachel and he assumed I never dated, and of course he's right, but I couldn't let him know that so I said I had a date, and when he asked me with whom, I couldn't think of anybody I could ask, but then I remembered you, so

I told him I had a date with you, and then I couldn't get away from him to call you and explain everything because he was coming out of the bathroom, and Patrick, if you don't stop kissing me, I'm going to cause you great bodily harm."

Abruptly Patrick lifted his head and stared at Jenny, as though everything had suddenly clicked in his head. "Then you don't have the hots for me?"

"Shhh!" Jenny grabbed Patrick's nape and pulled his head back down, so she could talk softly in his ear. "Keep it down. I don't want Matt to hear. And no, I don't have the hots for you." Responding to the drowned-dog look in Patrick's blue eyes, she said, "I'm sorry, Patrick. You're a good friend and my favorite student. I thought you wouldn't mind helping me out. Was I right?"

A wry grin appeared on Patrick's face. "You were right. Just what hypothesis is it we're going to prove here tonight, Professor Smith?"

"That I can be both a feminist and a desirable woman," Jenny replied. "In other words, Patrick, I want you to do exactly what you were doing. I just didn't want you to be hurt when you found out later that it was all for show."

"Sure, Professor Smith. I'm at your service. Let's see. Where was I?" He leaned down and tickled Jenny's ear with his tongue, causing her to laugh.

Matt's head came up at the sound of Jenny's husky laughter. He'd been wrong about her again. There certainly wasn't anything wrong with Jenny's sex appeal. Or Patrick's response to it. When she'd first shown up in his office, she'd been a series of contradictions. The buttoned-up blouse with the cat-clawed sleeves. Slinky black pants that fit her like a glove but hair twisted tight to her head without a strand out of place. She'd looked like a reference librarian on her way to a nightclub.

The woman dancing with Patrick was dressed to entice a man. Her skirt was slashed high to show off her long legs, and while no cleavage was actually revealed, the line of pearls drew the eye in that direction. She'd curled her hair—he'd seen it on the rollers—but it wasn't frizzy, just a riot of soft waves that bounced with the sway of her head.

Rachel tilted her hips into Matt's, demanding his attention. "I didn't know we were going to have company tonight, lover."

"As you can see," Matt said, letting the excess rope sway in the hand he held at her back, "I'm going to be tied up for the next few weeks."

Rachel pouted. She did it almost as well as she gushed. "I'd planned to spend the night with you. I suppose that isn't possible now."

"I'm afraid not." Much as it pained him, Matt was forced to admit that George's adjective, "dim-witted," probably fit Rachel better than it should. He'd never really noticed it before, but the contrast between Jenny's humor and intelligence and Rachel's chatter was striking. When he looked at Rachel as a person, rather than as a person of the opposite sex, she seemed singularly lacking in appeal.

That was when Matt knew he was in trouble. It wasn't that he minded having his consciousness raised—or whatever they called it—merely that he wasn't sure what would happen when he replaced Rachel with a woman like *Ms.* Smith. Jenny was opinionated, headstrong, stubborn, independent—not bad traits, he had to admit—except that he liked his women a little more pliable.

Of course, Jenny was also creative, fun to be with, and

not bad-looking. All right. She was stunning. So what? What good was beauty, if the woman wasn't going to let you near enough to enjoy it? Matt glanced sideways at Jenny and Patrick. On the other hand, Patrick certainly wasn't having any problems getting close.

Jenny tried not to watch as Matt kissed Rachel good night at her door, because the kiss went on and on. Just when she thought Matt might turn and come down the steps, Rachel caught him again. When he headed back toward the cab, Jenny turned quickly to Patrick and said, "You're going to have to kiss me good night, Patrick. And you're going to have to make it look good."

Patrick didn't smile. "Are you sure about this, Jenny? If the guy's such a jerk that he can't see—"

"Hello again, Matt," Jenny interrupted. "I take it Ms. Stephens didn't want the evening to end just yet."

"You took it right. *Miss* Stephens knows how to make a man feel like a man."

He was angry, but for the life of her, Jenny couldn't figure out why. "Is something wrong?"

He leaned over and muttered into Jenny's ear, "I'm reduced to double-dating like a high school kid and saying good night at the door. Then I'm going to be sleeping in the same room with a gorgeous woman I've promised not to touch. And you ask me if something's wrong?"

Before Jenny had time to reply, the cab arrived at the front stoop of her apartment. Matt jumped out and headed for the door. He didn't get far before the rope brought him up short.

"Looks like he doesn't want to see your good-night kiss, Jenny," Patrick said.

"He doesn't have much choice."

When they reached the front door, Matt opened it

and stepped inside, but he left the door open. "Are you coming?"

"She'll be with you in a moment," Patrick said.

When Patrick swept her into his arms, Jenny threw herself into the kiss. She found the interlude surprisingly enjoyable, but she didn't feel the same heightened awareness—or the frisson of desire—that had occurred with the mere brush of her fingertips against Matt's belly. She was glad she'd told Patrick ahead of time that their date was a pretense, because she could tell from the kiss that he felt more for her than she did for him.

"Thank you, Patrick," she murmured, when he finally broke the kiss. "It was a lovely evening."

"We'll do it again sometime," he promised. Then he ran back down the steps and jumped into the cab.

As they entered Jenny's apartment, Matt couldn't help noticing that her lips were still damp and a little swollen from the force of Patrick's kiss. He'd never wanted anything as much as he wanted to take her into his arms and erase the imprint of another man's kiss, another man's touch.

He closed the door behind them and said, "I want you, Jenny."

Matt hadn't realized he'd spoken aloud until Jenny turned to face him. Her pupils were dilated with desire, and she actually walked a step toward him, before she seemed to shake herself awake.

"What am I doing?" she said with a little laugh. "Whew! I must have had one too many glasses of wine this evening. I thought you said—"

"I did."

Jenny swallowed hard. She looked toward the bedroom door, then headed for the kitchen and a cup of tea, even though she was exhausted. The bedroom was no place to be with Matt until she could do something about the tremendous need that had turned her footsteps in his direction the instant he'd spoken. "I thought you wanted Rachel Stephens," she called over her shoulder.

Matt followed her into the kitchen, aware of what she was doing. "Rachel's the perfect date—for a male chauvinist pig."

Jenny couldn't help smiling. "You don't say."

"But she's no longer perfect for me."

"No?"

"At least, not for the next twenty-eight days." There was no need to let her know she already had him questioning his chauvinistic beliefs. He didn't want to give her an excuse to cut the project short. He had a feeling that the next twenty-eight days were going to be some of the most interesting of his life.

Matt didn't help her make the coffee, even though she fumbled through it, because it allowed him to watch her. When she finally set a cup in front of him, he sipped it in silence. It was awful coffee, but he drank it without complaint. She could learn to make coffee—or he could make it himself. He wondered if she could also learn to share herself with him, the way she'd shared herself with Russell this afternoon and with Patrick tonight. He couldn't remember the last time he'd been jealous of another man. And now he was jealous of her friendship with one man and her romance with another. It wasn't a feeling he wanted to cultivate.

Jenny was so tired her eyelids began to droop. "I've got to get some sleep," she said finally. "Are you ready for bed?"

The husky tremor in her voice sent a shiver through

Matt, but he'd promised her he could last for thirty days and, by God, he would. "You're right. It's late. Let's go to bed."

Jenny headed for the bedroom, slipping out of her heels as she went. She let them lie where they fell.

"You really must be tired to leave shoes strewn across the living room."

"Stuff it, Matt."

Matt laughed, and the tension that had kept them prisoner since they'd entered the apartment disappeared.

While Jenny stepped behind the screen to undress, Matt stripped down to his briefs, brushed his teeth, removed his contact lenses, and slipped under the sheets.

That was how Jenny found him when she came out from behind the screen. "That was quick."

"I've got my contact lens case here by the bed, just so there aren't any more mistakes, and I've brushed my teeth. What else is there?"

Jenny shook her head and padded to the bathroom door, closing it firmly behind her. She could sure use a set of male kidneys. When she'd been pregnant, she'd spent all her time in the bathroom. Tears misted her eyes at the thought of her daughter. If she'd only known then how little time she would have with Melody . . . She'd learned her lesson. She would never again take the moments she spent with someone she loved for granted.

The cold water she splashed on her face took care of her tears, and by the time she stepped from the bathroom, no residue of the painful past remained,

"You left toothpaste in the sink," she said.

Matt yawned. "I'll get it tomorrow morning, along with the laundry on the floor."

Jenny slipped into bed and reached for her book.

"You're not going to read, are you?"

"I was. I guess I won't, if it's going to bother you."

"It's going to bother me." Matt rolled over and closed his eyes. "Let's turn out the light, Jenny, and get some sleep. It's past two in the morning."

"I win!" Jenny crowed.

"What?"

When Matt opened his eyes enough to see her, she was standing triumphantly beside her bed, her arms crossed under her breasts, and a huge grin on her face. "I didn't mention the time once today. You're the one who brought it up first."

Matt swore under his breath. "I suppose you want to collect on your bet tomorrow."

"Why not? It'll be good practice for you, since we have to fly to San Francisco tomorrow evening. You can't smoke on the plane anyway."

"Let's talk about it tomorrow," he said.

Jenny was happy to avoid an argument, especially since they'd been getting along so well all day. It was also the first time in a long time that she'd enjoyed a day without contemplating the fragility of life. She owed Matt a debt of gratitude for that. But in order to thank him, she'd have to explain what had bound her to the clock in the first place. After just two days with Matt, she wasn't ready to bare her soul to him. Despite the fact that she was living with him, despite the fact that she liked him—and desired him—they were virtual strangers. She would just have to wait and see whether Matt Benson turned out to be the kind of person to whom she could confide her deepest thoughts.

CHAPTER ELEVEN

Jenny had known sleep wouldn't come easily, but she'd counted on getting a full eight hours' rest once she finally drifted off. The tug on her waist at the break of dawn proved she was wrong. She caught a glimpse of Matt's shoulders as he was doing his push-ups. She turned over and hid her face in the pillow, but she could still see the play of his muscles in her mind's eye and smell the not-unpleasant odor of his sweat-dampened flesh.

The next thing she knew, Matt's voice rasped in her ear, "Would you mind getting into my bed, Jenny?"

She sat up abruptly, saw he was wearing no more than a towel, and clamped her eyes shut. "Don't forget the toothpaste in the sink," she muttered as she complied, careful not to open her eyes.

The tension between them was suddenly back.

Jenny was aware of Matt every moment during the very long day that followed, because neither of them had work to distract them. She filled the time reading, when she wasn't packing for their trip to the west coast. Matt seemed as restless as she felt, pacing like a caged animal. She was relieved when the time finally came to take a cab to the airport for their evening flight.

Jenny had called ahead to the airport to say that she and Matt would be tied together with a rope and to explain the nature of her project. Although there were a few stares at the security gate, they made it through with a minimum of fuss.

Things didn't go quite so smoothly once they got to San Francisco. Jenny had booked reservations at a hotel far enough in advance to make sure they'd have twin beds, but it seemed there had been some mix-up, and the only room left had a king-size bed. Jenny would just as soon have gone to another hotel, but with the three-hour time difference, it was already midnight in New York, and they would have a tough time finding last-minute accommodations at nine o'clock on a Saturday night.

When the young man at the registration desk confirmed that nothing else was available, Jenny made a decision. "We'll take it."

She breathed a sigh of relief when she saw the bed. It was huge. She glanced surreptitiously at Matt. He wasn't chewing the inside of his cheek anymore, something that had begun when he'd heard they'd be sharing a bed. Surely they could manage to sleep together in such a big bed without accidentally touching. Just in case, she planned to bundle the bedspread between them.

"You can have the bathroom first," Matt said.

"All right." It suddenly dawned on Jenny that the bathroom was considerably farther from the bed here than in her apartment. In fact, if she had reason to use the facilities during the night, as she sometimes did, she'd have to wake Matt up to do it. In the future, she realized she would need to ask for more details about the rooms they had to share.

Matt was sitting in the chair at the small writing table when Jenny came out of the bathroom. She was wearing one of her T-shirts with the side slit to accommodate the rope, and he caught a glimpse of her long legs as she approached.

"I'm done," she said.

"I won't be long," he said, heading for the bathroom. He paused at the door and said, "You know, we really ought to do something to stay awake for another hour or so, or our inner clocks are going to be very confused at dawn."

"What did you have in mind?"

"How about a glass of wine on the balcony?"

Jenny looked at the sliding glass door that led to a balcony with a decent view of the bay and some of the old Victorian houses that were a San Francisco landmark. "That sounds lovely. I'll call down—"

"I've already ordered from room service. You can get the door, if they come while I'm in the bathroom."

The wine and a selection of cheeses and fruit came almost the moment Matt disappeared into the bathroom, and Jenny had the bellboy set up a table for them on the balcony. The bellboy ignored the rope that led from Jenny's waist into the bathroom with a nonchalance Jenny thought bellboys the world over must practice to perfection.

When Matt rejoined her, he was wearing a pair of blue cotton pajama bottoms that rode low on his hips.

"So that's what was in the package you got today," Jenny said, admiring the way the cotton hugged his narrow hips.

"I figured I'd better cover up while we're on the road."

If he thought he was less sexually attractive, Jenny thought as she let her eyes roam his body, he was wrong. His hair was still damp from the shower, and he smelled of soap and herbal shampoo. She found Matt in half a set of pajamas difficult to ignore. She clenched her teeth to keep from telling him how good he looked.

"Shall we?" He gestured toward the balcony, and Jenny hurried ahead of him in an attempt to escape the scent and the sight of him.

The light evening breeze was cool, but not cold, and Jenny found the fog enchanting, probably because she didn't have to drive in it. The wine was crisp and dry, the cheese exotic, the fruit sweet, and the company was . . . distracting.

Jenny was surprised when Matt said, "Tell me about your marriage."

The silence grew while she thought about how to answer him. At last she said, "It didn't end up being an altogether pleasant experience."

"What went wrong?"

Jenny took a deep breath and let it out. "I got pregnant, Sam lost his job, and I got promoted, in that order."

"I didn't know you had a child."

"I don't." Jenny hadn't meant to be curt, but she wasn't ready to talk about Melody.

"So you chose your career over having children?"

"No. . . I . . . It's a long story."

"I've got time," he said, taking a sip of wine.

To avoid answering, Jenny said, "It's your turn to answer a question."

"Shoot."

"What went wrong with your marriage?"

Matt gave a low laugh and shook his head. "It's funny, but the whole time I was growing up, I always swore I wouldn't marry a woman like my mother. I wanted a woman who'd be willing to stay home and take care of the children, while I went out and earned a living. What I didn't realize was all those years I'd resented my mother for not being there, I'd also admired her for the work she did that took her away from us.

"When Adrienne—my wife—came along, I was so captivated by her intelligence, her ambition, her energy . . . I told myself it would work out."

"But it didn't."

"When I suggested it might be time we started a family, Adrienne informed me, in no uncertain terms, that children weren't a part of her future."

"Didn't you discuss having kids before you got married?"

"Of course we did. Adrienne expressed some reservations, but fool that I am, I thought she would change her mind—or that I would change it for her."

"I'm sorry," Jenny said.

Matt sighed. "I made a mistake, and we both got hurt by it."

"Why aren't you married to a housewife now, with three kids and another on the way?"

"I haven't found the right woman. I'm not sure I ever will."

Jenny wondered if all the women he dated were like Rachel. She couldn't picture Rachel playing the happy housewife. But then, she couldn't picture herself in that role, either. "I think women today want more than a single narrow role in a man's life—or in their own lives, for that matter. I know I do. I suppose we women can't have it all—a career and the joy of being a wife and mother—without compromising somewhere. But there has to be a way to balance things, so we can be fulfilled in as many areas of our lives as possible."

"The world has changed," Matt conceded. "I guess I'm going to have to change with it."

"It would be nice to marry an enlightened man, someone who'd be happy to have a wife who was also a working mother. That wasn't my experience."

"If you want to be a wife and mother, why all this performance art with a feminist political theme? It doesn't make sense."

"I had a husband like you," Jenny explained. "Before you flatter yourself that you're the kind of man I'd pick to marry, you should know that I found being married to a male chauvinist more than a little stifling. There's a fine line between a man who cares for a woman, and one who's bent on taking care of her. I want a man who cares, but who'll accept me as an equal partner."

"Is that where you got the 'separate but equal' concept for this project?"

"I suppose so."

"What other attributes will this perfect marriage partner have?"

"I guess you saw all the romance novels on my bookshelf."

Matt nodded.

"In every one there's a hero who's sensitive and thoughtful, but also strong—or maybe self-confident—enough to let the heroine be all she's destined to be. Is it so wrong to wish for a man like that in real life?"

"Real people have flaws. They're not perfect."

"Are you telling me I'm not going to find a sensitive, self-confident man out there somewhere?"

Matt made a face. "Guess you've got me there. If I say no, I denigrate the whole male sex. If I say yes, where does that leave us male chauvinist pigs?"

Jenny laughed. "You don't want to hear my answer to that. Honestly, Matt, I wouldn't have believed I could have such a rational discussion with someone as biased as you are against the female sex."

"I must admit, you're the first liberated woman who's made any sense to me. Perhaps, on that convivial note, we should head for bed."

Jenny suddenly realized that going to bed meant going to bed *together*. The king-size bed was huge, but she still felt anxious about sleeping in the same space as Matt.

After he ripped the covers back, Jenny gathered up the spread and rolled it into a tube long enough to run from the head to the foot of the mattress. "This side is mine. That side is yours. And the middle is no-man's land. Got it, Benson?"

"Got it, Smith."

Once he was in bed, Matt couldn't sleep. There was an intimacy in the sleeping arrangements that wasn't conducive to rest. He could tell Jenny wasn't asleep, since she kept tossing and turning like a cat circling a basket, trying to find a comfortable spot.

Finally he said, "Do you really think these performances will make any difference in the greater scheme of things?"

Jenny could barely make out Matt's features in the moonlight coming through the sliding glass door. "If I didn't think so, I wouldn't do it."

Matt didn't want to talk, he wanted to touch. But that was forbidden. He'd told Jenny she could trust him to keep his hands to himself. If he wasn't careful, he was going to do something he'd regret. He gave an irritated huff, pulled the blanket up over his shoulder, and said, "Good night, Jenny."

"Good night, Matt." A moment later she said in a soft voice, "I like your choice of pajamas."

Matt grinned. It seemed Miss Keep-Your-Hands-to-Yourself wasn't as unaware of the differences between the sexes as she wanted him to think. His grin faded as he let himself wonder what it would have been like if he'd married a woman like Jenny. She'd said she wanted to fit a traditional female role, and in the same breath, that she wanted a partner who would be her equal. Were the two desires so irreconcilable? He knew from his past marriage that things were rarely ever equal between spouses. Could he give a woman the kind of freedom and support Jenny had said she needed to be happy? Matt sighed. Talk about moot issues. He was a chauvinist. She was a feminist. And never the twain shall meet.

Jenny heard Matt's sigh and knew exactly how he felt. There weren't any easy answers when it came to resolving such basic differences as the two of them held. But there was no reason she couldn't believe in miracles. Jenny smiled to herself. She was pretty sure it was going to take a miracle to get rid of Matt's *oink*.

CHAPTER TWELVE

"I've never felt so humiliated in my entire life!"

They were on the plane home to New York from San Francisco, and Jenny was trying her best to calm Matt down, without much success. "It's over and done with now. Just forget it happened."

"I'll never be able to face my colleagues again."

"Come on, Matt. It can't be that bad."

"Not that bad? Jerry Vanderwood, the critic from *Focus on Art*—our major competitor on the West Coast—was standing there laughing. Laughing!"

"Well, it *was* pretty funny." Jenny faked a cough and hid her grin behind her hand.

"If I'd known what you had planned, I never would have gone. How could you, Jenny?"

Jenny squelched the flicker of guilt she felt at Matt's accusation. A typical American living room had been recreated in a roped-off section of the gallery. At the moment in question, Jenny had been lying on the couch reading a book, and Matt had been sitting on the floor beside her, his legs stretched out in front of him, watching television. "I knew the gallery was going to invite schoolchildren, but how could I know that little girl would be so outspoken? All she did—"

"All she did was make a fool of me!"

"Where's your sense of humor? All she said was that you looked cute, just like her puppy when he was on his leash. She didn't know that critic was standing right beside her." Jenny could still hear the childish voice piping up, "My puppy likes to watch television, too."

A strangled sound issued from Matt's throat.

Fortunately, the flight attendant interrupted to ask, "Would either of you like something to drink?"

"I'd like some white wine," Jenny said.

"Jack Daniel's," Matt snarled. "And keep it coming."

By the time they reached New York, he seemed less agitated, but it was hard to tell, because he hadn't spoken for the rest of the trip.

Jenny knew the male ego was a fragile thing, but she'd never suspected Matt's could be crushed so easily. He was more vulnerable than she'd suspected, and she hoped that what had happened in San Francisco wasn't going to cause him to renege on his commitment to her project.

She gave directions to the cabbie, who drove them back to her apartment. Matt followed her upstairs without a word and plopped down on the bed closest to the bathroom, throwing his forearm over his face with great melodrama.

By the time Jenny got out of the bathroom, Matt was sitting up in bed with the sheet draped across his waist.

He met her gaze and said, "We have to talk."

Jenny crossed to her bed and climbed in before she turned to Matt, her muscles tensed for the blow she felt sure was coming. "All right. Go ahead."

"I want to apologize. I guess I overreacted."

Jenny's rigid shoulders slumped in relief. "Does this mean you aren't backing out of the project?"

Matt slid his feet onto the floor and leaned forward with his elbows on his knees, making Jenny aware of his broad chest and narrow waist.

He shot her a chagrined smile. "I'd have to be a fool to give up the chance of spending the next twenty-six days—and nights—with you."

Jenny would have laughed, except she was too aware of the sexual tension arcing between them. "You're no kind of fool, Matt. Anyone can see that."

"Can you, Jenny?"

Jenny nodded, because speaking would have revealed how flustered she was by Matt's intense gaze.

"Then perhaps you'll agree to go to a football game with me on Thursday."

"What?" She was surprised at the abrupt change of subject—from her project to football.

"I have tickets for the Jets game on Thursday night. Want to go?"

Jenny laughed, this time at herself, for thinking Matt had been, even for a brief moment, sexually attracted to her. "You didn't have to ask. You know I have to go anyway."

"I want you to be my date."

"Your date?"

Jenny looked stunned, and Matt thought maybe he'd gone too far. He was on the verge of withdrawing his request when she drawled. "Why, Mr. Benson, I do believe you're hustling a feminist."

Matt laughed. "Why, *Ms.* Smith, I do believe you're

right."

That encounter set the tone for the rest of the week, which passed more pleasantly than Jenny could have hoped.

The reviews from the San Francisco newspapers were, if not glowing, at least positive. Jenny had to wait another week for the review from *Focus on Art,* but if the newspaper coverage was any guide, she didn't have anything to worry about. She read to Matt:

. . . part of the critic's job is to discern whether performance art speaks to the audience for which it is intended. In Separate but Equal, *artist Jennifer Smith asks us to believe a premise that many would not espouse wholeheartedly today. By her choice of subject matter alone, she forces us to confront our consciences on the matter of sexual equality. If she does no more than that, she has done enough.*

"Don't get your hopes up that Jerry Vanderwood will be so supportive," Matt warned. "He's a dyed-in-the-wool male chauvinist."

"And you're not?"

"No, I donned my hair shirt later in life."

Jenny was silent for a moment while she considered what Matt had just admitted. If what he said was true, perhaps it was possible for him to shed his prejudice as easily as doffing a wool coat when springtime came around again. "At any rate," Jenny said, "I'm not going to mope around all week worrying about it. It's enough of a coup for me to have simply gotten him to come in the first place."

In Tuesday's class, Jenny was impressed with Matt's perceptive contributions to the assignment she'd given her students, asking them which should be saved from a fire: an old man or Da Vinci's *Mona Lisa?*

After the students had given their initial answers, Matt suggested they alter the problem slightly. *What if the man was very ill and was going to die anyway?* Which would they save? Or *What if you had to choose between saving the* Mona Lisa *or a cat?* As a living being, did the cat deserve more consideration than a priceless work of art? Or did the fact that it was "only a cat" make its life of negligible value?

The discussion had been lively, and Matt helped her students work toward the answer Jenny had reached long ago: An artist shouldn't sacrifice everything—marriage, family, happiness, even hearth and home—for art. Being an artist was important, but having a good life was even more so.

She wasn't really surprised that Matt had apparently come to the same conclusion as she had, but she was surprised that a chauvinist and a feminist had such a fundamental belief in common. It caused her to see him in a very different light. It made her want to get to know him better. Luckily, she had the time—and the proximity—to do exactly that.

CHAPTER THIRTEEN

Matt was pleasantly surprised on Thursday to discover that Jenny was a Jets fan. "You never told me you love football," he shouted over the crowd noise in New Jersey's Meadowlands complex.

"You never asked!" she shouted back with a grin. She jumped up excitedly as the wide receiver caught a long bomb. "Did you see that?" she yelled. "Wow! First and goal on the three-yard line. Go, Jets!"

Matt was once again stymied by the incongruities in Jenny's behavior. Feminists weren't supposed to enjoy football. Were they?

Later that evening in bed, Jenny was still bubbly with excitement. "What a game! I couldn't believe that pass in the fourth quarter. We'll be seeing the run that followed it for the next twenty years when they do the recaps on TV."

"Where did you learn to like football?" Matt asked

"My father loved the game. I guess I started watching

at his knee and came to love it as much as he did." Jenny shot him a look filled with mischief. "Lots of women love football, Matt. We can be just as bloodthirsty and competitive as any man."

"But you don't look like—"

"People rarely fit pigeonholes. That's one of the reasons I wanted you to spend time with me on this project, so you could see how true that is of both men and women."

"Is Russell one of those people who doesn't fit a pigeonhole?" Matt asked.

Although the question had come out of left field, Jenny sensed the underlying curiosity and concern about her relationship with her business partner. "Russell's life hasn't been predictable, if that's what you're asking. He used to be a football player, a good one. He got injured and had to leave the game. He's one of those people who never learned the lesson I'm trying to teach my students by making them choose between "life" and "art" in a fictitious scenario. He sacrificed everything for the game, and when he couldn't play anymore, he had nothing left to live for. It took him a long time to figure out his life after football.

"It was especially hard, because what he discovered he wanted to do wasn't something one expects of an ex-football player. He took a lot of ribbing from some of his former teammates. But an equal number stood by him, and now he's a successful, happy human being."

"How much did you personally have to do with Russell's self-discovery?"

"Not much, really. When he was looking for a studio I had a whole loft to myself and—"

"You offered to share it with him. That was very

generous, Jenny. Not at all competitive and bloodthirsty."

She flushed. "I've never been sorry."

"I never suggested you were."

The awkward strain between them suddenly returned. Jenny was once again conscious of the fact that she was sharing her bedroom with a man she'd known only seven days. After spending day and night together all that time, she could hardly call Matt a stranger. Yet there were so many things they didn't know about each other, so many spots of quicksand that could catch them unawares, and leave them sinking into the mire.

Jenny shivered and pulled the sheet up over her shoulders.

"Are you cold?"

"No, I just . . ." Jenny wasn't sure she could explain her conflicting feelings. So she didn't try. Instead she said, "I'm tired. It's been a long day. Good night, Matt."

"Good night, Jenny."

Matt's raspy voice sent another shiver down Jenny's spine. He'd acted the role of friend all week, but something else was happening between them as well. More than once she'd seen a look in his eyes that was more than "friendly." A look that sent a frisson of expectation down her spine.

Matt stared at the cold shoulder Jenny had turned on him. What had happened to create the chill in the air between them? He hadn't consciously said or done anything provocative, had he? He'd merely let her see that he admired her, had even spoken of his admiration. Surely friends could show their esteem for one another. And Jenny *was* his friend, at least as much as someone could be on seven days' acquaintance. He was trying hard not to want more from her, but it wasn't easy.

The truth of the matter was, he'd spent a lot of time lately imagining himself as Jenny Smith's lover. Considering the fact that he'd promised not to touch her for an endlessly long time to come, he'd be better off thinking about something—anything—else. That would have been a lot easier if he was tied to the focus of his thoughts without any hope of escape. He hadn't considered what it would mean to spend thirty long days—and very long nights—without touching the object of his desire.

Matt shook his head, chagrined at himself for getting into this situation in the first place. If he didn't admire—and respect—Jenny so much, he'd be out of here in a heartbeat. But he'd made a commitment. What he had to do now was give her the time to prove her thesis. And do his best to convince her that she was dead wrong.

CHAPTER FOURTEEN

Their fragile friendship was sorely tested by the trip to the Chicago gallery over the weekend, which was a nightmare of mishaps. The plane was delayed out of Kennedy, then delayed again before it could land at O'Hare. The hotel room had double beds, all right, but Jenny had eaten something on the plane that disagreed with her stomach, so Matt spent most of the night sitting outside the bathroom door, which was on the opposite side of the room from their beds.

There was a cold snap in Chicago, and neither Jenny nor Matt had brought cold-weather clothes. The gallery wasn't heated, so they spent an uncomfortable afternoon being ogled by patrons bundled up in hats and sweaters. Jenny suffered in silence through the performance, then let Matt drag her back to the airport, where they waited in vain for a flight that was finally canceled. They ended up taking a cab to a hotel located near the airport.

In the hotel's sundry shop Jenny found a copy of

the most recent *Focus on Art.* She forced herself to wait until they were in their room to open the magazine and read the review of *Separate but Equal.* Jerry Vanderwood's critique was scathing.

Matt could see from Jenny's grim features that the review wasn't good. He took the magazine from her and read, "'To a world full of tripe, performance artist Jennifer Smith has added yet another piece of feminist rubbish.'" It was strictly downhill from there.

"I'm sorry, Jenny," Matt said when he'd finished reading it. He closed the distance between them until he was standing next to her in the middle of the room. "It's just one opinion."

"But an important one," she replied bitterly. "You said yourself, he's your major competition. That means he has a large readership. Oh, Matt! Can he possibly be right?"

"That doesn't sound like the Jenny I've known for the past thirteen days. Where's your fighting spirit?" He yearned to reach out and comfort her, to lift her chin and infuse her with some of his strength. He wondered if she'd felt this bad when she'd read his review of *Woman at a Party.* He hoped not. She looked absolutely miserable. "You can't let a little thing like this get you down."

"I'm tired, Matt. Please, would you turn down the sheets? I think if I don't lie down, I'm going to topple over."

Her cheeks looked feverishly pink to Matt. "Are you sure you don't have a temperature?" He started to lay his hand on Jenny's brow, and at the last second realized what he was doing and stopped himself. Jenny was too far gone even to notice.

In fact, she was so far gone that she undressed right there beside the bed, seemingly unaware that she was exposing the flat plane of her stomach above her silk bikini panties and the rosy nipples barely hidden by her lace bra.

Matt slapped down his unruly libido and tucked Jenny into bed, resisting the temptation to climb in after her.

"Did I ever tell you," Jenny murmured, "what I thought when I first saw you?"

Matt wondered just how sick she was. When she opened her eyes, they were feverishly bright. "No. You never did. Are you going to tell me now?"

"Yes." Jenny's eyes closed, her lush lashes resting against her cheeks. She was practically asleep, Matt realized.

"You looked like the hero in one of my romance novels. But you were so mean! Once I got to know you," she murmured, "I realized you weren't a creep after all."

"A creep?" Matt sputtered.

Jenny had the sheet pulled up to her chin. She was mumbling, but somehow, he had no trouble understanding her next comment.

"After I read your review of *Woman at a Party* I called you a lot of names. 'Creep' was one of the nicer ones."

"But I reminded you of a hero when you met me?"

"You're very handsome."

That was something, at least, Matt thought wryly. But she wasn't done.

"I suppose one of the nice things about being half of a couple is that when one half is down the other half can . . . take up . . . the slack."

As she spoke, Jenny slowly but surely collected the rope that lay between them until Matt's face was inches from hers.

What are you doing?

I'm so tired of keeping my distance. I want him to kiss me. I want him to hold me in his arms.

What about your project, Jenny?

To hell with it! I can't stand the tension anymore.

You '11 regret this tomorrow.

Jenny ignored the little voice that warned her she was making a mistake. Her eyes focused on Matt's mouth, which had parted, and she watched avidly as his tongue slowly dampened his lower lip. Then her eyes met his, and she found all the need she was experiencing herself.

Matt recognized Jenny's sensual response to his gaze. His body was responding with equal alacrity. "Jenny, we can't do this."

"Why not?"

"You'll be sorry in the morning."

"No, I won't. Please, Matt."

Matt resisted the urge to nibble on Jenny's pouting lower lip. He lowered his head until he could feel Jenny's breath on his face. Then something stopped him. Touching Jenny now would mean the end of any chance for a retraction of his negative review.

A small voice inside him argued, *She asked you to touch her. She begged, just the way you knew she would. So, kiss her. Do it now!*

Abruptly, Matt jerked away. Making the rational choice to keep his distance did nothing to calm the throbbing need he felt. But he knew it was the right choice. "I must be crazy," he said, "but I can't take advantage of you like this. You're exhausted. You're hurting. You don't know what you're doing."

Jenny felt the hot tears on her cheeks and turned onto her side away from Matt. Surely she couldn't be crying because Matthew Benson, chauvinist, destroyer of artistic careers, heartless creep—who'd most recently been acting suspiciously like the hero of her dreams—hadn't wanted to make love to her.

CHAPTER FIFTEEN

They were both wan with fatigue when they boarded the plane the next morning for New York.

Jenny had spent the night regretting her lamentable lapse in control.

Matt had spent the night regretting his disgusting sense of nobility.

"I have an exhibit to review this afternoon," he announced as the plane was landing at Kennedy.

Jenny winced at the thought of the long day ahead. She hadn't slept the previous night, and she was pretty sure Matt hadn't either. Yet there was no way to get a respite from one another's company. How long could they last like this?

By the time they got back to her apartment, after attending the exhibit, they didn't speak, just headed for the bedroom, which had become a haven for them both.

"It's good to be home," Matt said.

Jenny groaned with relief as she slid off her shoes.

"Yes, it is. We'd better get to bed. I've got class early tomorrow."

"Fourteen days down after tomorrow, sixteen to go. I'll be glad when this damned project is over."

That comment set the tone for the coming week. Neither of them slept well, so their fatigue built to monumental proportions. Their appetites suffered. Everything was an irritant, abrading the fragile shell of polite behavior that kept them from attacking each other physically. Verbally, all bets were off.

"You left toothpaste in the sink again."

"If it bothers you so much, wipe it up."

"Will you please pick up your blasted undershorts!"

"Step over them."

"Is this the best coffee you can make?"

"If it tastes like poison, it's probably because I wish it was."

Jenny knew she was being a shrew, but there didn't seem to be anything she could do about it. Neither one of them had been acting much like a rational adult for the past few days. She could find no other explanation for her behavior than the fact that it was driving her crazy being no farther than ten feet away from a man she found sexually attractive—but couldn't touch.

Matt was down to his last shred of tolerance. He thought perhaps what they both needed was a change of scene. "We're going to have dinner at my house tonight."

"I didn't know you had a house," Jenny snapped.

Matt bit back a sharp retort and responded calmly, "Well, I do. We can take the train from Penn station and be on Long Island in half an hour." Thinking Jenny might be reluctant to go and desperate to get her to agree, he added, "I have to go there anyway to pick up the artist's supplies I need for the United Way benefit next Saturday. We might as well do that now."

"What artist's supplies? What United Way benefit?"

"I thought I told you about it."

"No, you didn't."

Matt bit back a terrible word he had no business saying in front of a lady. Instead, he carefully explained, "There's a United Way benefit for supporters of the arts. I've agreed to sell caricatures of the personalities who attend, with the proceeds going to the United Way."

"I didn't know you did caricatures."

"There's a lot you don't know about me," he replied. "We'll spend tonight at my place and catch the train back into the city tomorrow in plenty of time to make our flight to Houston. Want to go?"

Jenny was feeling petulant enough to say no, but what came out was, "Sure."

They caught the train that afternoon, picking up Matt's car where he'd left it parked near the station and driving the rest of the way to his house, which was located on a tree-shaded lane in Roslyn Heights. It was a split-level, with a big bay window in front. Tasteful, comfortable, just the sort of suburban home where one might find a wife, 2.3 children, and a dog. In Matt's case, he only had the dog.

"That's Spot," Matt said as he explained the appearance of an excited dalmatian barking at the fence. "My neighbor's been taking care of him for me, while I've been staying in the city with you."

Matt opened the door and gestured Jenny inside ahead of him. She stopped at the entry to the living room and stared at her surroundings in awe. The furniture consisted of large, masculine pieces in earth tones, from buff brown to burnt sienna. The room had a slightly cluttered, lived-in look. Old gallery programs were scattered everywhere. A beer can sat on the coffee table, and a baseball cap was perched on the lamp shade. "It's so . . . warm."

The house had been closed up, and Matt moved quickly to adjust the climate control. "It'll cool off soon."

Jenny turned and caught the end of what he was saying. "I meant, your home, it's so cozy. It gives me a warm feeling inside."

Matt smiled at Jenny, a smile that offered all the warmth of the man and melted the coldness that had existed between them all week. "Come on. Let me show you the rest of the place."

"How many bedrooms do you have?"

"Three upstairs, one downstairs. I use the downstairs bedroom for guests. Although, in this case, I guess you'll have to stay upstairs with me," Matt said with the first grin that had touched his face in a week.

Jenny headed straight for the painting of a New England fall landscape that had been hung above the fireplace. It was signed "Benson." "This is a wonderful, Matt." She turned to face him. "Why did you quit?"

He shrugged. "I knew I'd never be great. Being good wasn't good enough for me." Uncomfortable with Jenny's questioning, he said, "Do you want a tour or not?"

Hoping to maintain the temporary truce between them, Jenny quickly said, "Let's go."

When she entered an upstairs bedroom obviously intended for children, Jenny strongly felt the loss of her daughter. She turned to Matt and said, "I'm surprised you have a space like this, when your wife didn't want to have children. This room—"

"My nieces and nephews stay here when they come to

visit," Matt interrupted.

Jenny followed Matt to his bedroom. The first thing she noticed was the king-size bed. On the opposite side of the room, a desk sat facing a large picture window that opened on a backyard barbecue and a pool.

"I planned to watch my kids playing in the backyard from here," Matt said.

"Why did you keep the house?" Jenny asked. "After you divorced, I mean. Isn't it a little large for a single man?"

Matt looked sheepish. "I guess I never gave up hoping that someday I'd fill it with my kids." He shoved a hand through his hair, leaving it askew, and revealing his discomfort with such a personal topic. "That's enough of that. I'm hungry."

"Is the kitchen stocked?"

"We ought to be able to throw something together out of what's in the freezer."

They ate T-bone steaks by candlelight in the dining room, washing it down with a cabernet sauvignon.

"I wish it were cooler," Matt said. "I'd light a fire, and we could retire to the living room with a brandy."

"We can still have the brandy, can't we?" Jenny asked, catching his glance over the rim of her wine glass.

He swallowed hard. The tension they'd fought all week had changed. He wasn't sure what was happening between them; he only knew he was damned confused. "Sure. Just let me clean up—"

"We can do that together later, can't we?" She rose and sauntered into the living room, giving Matt a "come hither" look as she passed him, and then giving a tug on the rope.

If he hadn't known better, Matt would have thought

that Jenny was making a pass at him. But, of course, it had to be his imagination.

Jenny settled herself on the couch and waited for Matt to pour their brandies. Everything she'd ever wanted from a home was in this house, including a man who wanted children. So what was she going to do about it?

CHAPTER SIXTEEN

Matt didn't know exactly what was going on in Jenny's head, but he wasn't about to argue with the intimate scene she'd arranged—the two of them lounging on the couch, soft candlelight, and a good glass of brandy. Jenny was a beautiful woman, and he was more than willing to satisfy any urges she wanted satisfied.

The problem was her contradictory signals.

He took advantage of a "yes" signal to move closer to her on the couch. The instant he did, she backed away from him.

Definitely a "no."

Before he had a chance to get discouraged, she slipped off the couch to a spot on the floor beside him, then turned to face him, her hands laced together on the couch a bare inch from his thigh.

That was a "yes."

But as he edged his thigh closer to her hand, she shifted again, this time to sprawl back against a hassock, with her legs spread wide on either side of his feet.

Was that a "yes" or a "no?"

Matt was a patient man, and he'd been teased by the best of them. But he'd been aroused even before he'd come into the room with Jenny, and the sight of her sprawled spread-legged across from him had left him hard and ready. He wanted her to make up her mind.

There were several more "yes" overtures, all of which Matt answered, so that when the "I've changed my mind about the whole thing" signal came, it tipped him over the edge.

"That's it!"

"What's wrong?"

"Don't act innocent, Jenny. You know damn well what's wrong!"

"I don't," she protested.

Matt stuck a finger under Jenny's nose and said, "If I touch you without your say-so I have to print a retraction. But you've been doing your damnedest to make sure I touch you."

"I haven't."

"If you choose to keep yourself tied up in sexual knots, that's your business, but don't play games with me."

"I wasn't playing," she protested.

Matt was on a roll, and he wasn't about to let Jenny's helpless, innocent act get in the way of his rampage. "If you want to deny yourself the pleasure of sex for the rest of your life, fine."

"I never—"

"After this little show, all I can say is that your husband must have been glad to be rid of you."

"It wasn't me Sam wanted to be rid of, it was our

baby!" Jenny snapped.

Matt exhaled a deep sigh, filling the terrible silence. "Jenny, I didn't know. I thought—"

Tears suddenly brimmed in her eyes.

"I'm sorry," Matt said.

Caught up as she was in the nightmare of the past, the words just tumbled out of Jenny. "He said to get rid of her, but I didn't. I kept her, and I loved her until she . . . until she died." Her breath caught on a sob, and she turned away from Matt, hiding her face in her hands.

Matt suspected that only extreme agitation—the result of innocence in the face of his accusations—could have driven her to reveal the truth about her marriage. And her child. How devastating that must have been for her. How did you comfort someone for such a terrible tragedy? He wasn't sure what to say. So he said nothing.

In the silence that followed, Matt had time to realize that he hadn't been angry with Jenny because she'd said no. A lot of women had said no in the past, and he hadn't flown off the handle. It occurred to him that the reason he'd been so angry was because he didn't know whether she really wanted him, or whether she'd been using him to get her damned retraction. While his feelings—and he wasn't willing to define them too carefully—were genuine, he feared hers weren't.

He crouched down, careful not to brush against her, and offered the only solace he could. "If you want to talk about it, I'm here to listen."

Jenny tucked her legs beneath her as she turned warily toward Matt. She reached for her glass of brandy and took a swallow, as she considered whether to share something she'd kept hidden for a very long time. "All right," she said at last.

Matt sat down beside her, so they were both on the floor, leaning back against the couch. Matt watched as she ran her fingers agitatedly through her hair, smoothed her rumpled blouse, and clasped her hands together with her fingers intertwined. Finally she spoke.

"The demand for an abortion was the reason I divorced my husband," she began. "Sam wasn't ready for children, so I raised Melody by myself. She was four years old when she died. That was five years ago." Jenny took another sip of brandy. "She had a rare kind of childhood leukemia. The symptoms didn't show up right away. By the time they did, the doctors didn't give me much hope. They told me she might have six months. She only had four."

Matt watched helplessly as the tears pooled in Jenny's eyes and spilled over. Suddenly, he understood her obsession with time. Despite the tragedy she'd unfolded for him, he was filled with hope. Because the fact that Jenny had lost her child meant that at some point she'd made the choice to become a mother. He wanted to hold her in his arms and soothe away her pain, but he couldn't even reach out a hand in comfort. Words didn't seem like enough, but they were all he was allowed.

"I'm . . . " He cleared his throat and tried again. "I'm so sorry, Jenny."

He didn't know whether she heard him or not. She seemed to be caught in a web of painful memories. He kept his promise and listened as she admitted, "I don't think about Melody all the time anymore. But every once in a while, something will trigger a memory, and she's there, laughing, smiling, telling me how much she loves me . . . being brave for Mommy."

Matt couldn't help himself. He reached out to her.

"Don't! Don't touch me," she rasped, shrinking away from his outstretched hands.

"Jenny, let me share the hurt. Let me—"

"No. You said you wouldn't touch me unless I asked you to, Matt. My project—"

"Damn your project! Are you forgetting your own lessons?" he retorted. "Or was that all just so much rhetoric? I thought you believed what you taught. *Art is important, but life is more important.* Let me help, Jenny."

She swiped at the tears on her face but remained distant.

"At least tell me what I can do to help, if I can't touch you."

His hoarse plea reached her at last, and Jenny turned and focused on his compassionate gray eyes, feeling a wave of comfort flowing over her. "I think you already have helped, simply by listening. I've never told anyone else what I just told you. I guess I needed to get all that out, but somehow there was never anybody I wanted to tell."

"I'm glad you chose me."

"Me, too," Jenny said with a watery smile. "Melody's buried in a cemetery outside Houston. I'd like to go visit her when we're there over the weekend."

"Sure." Matt reached out to take her brandy snifter, careful not to brush her hand. "Come on. It's time for bed. We've got to get up early tomorrow to catch the train back into the city."

He led her upstairs and waited patiently outside the bathroom door until she'd changed into her T-shirt. Then he stepped into the bathroom himself. When he came out he was wearing both the top and bottom of a pair of blue cotton pajamas.

"Pajamas?"

"It's going to be hard enough to sleep in this bed tonight without touching you. I need all the help I can get."

Jenny hadn't forgotten the scene that had resulted from her ambivalence toward having Matt touch her. She quickly slipped under the covers, careful not to tease him further. She turned on her side, facing away from him, and he did the same with her. The vast expanse of the king-size bed yawned like an abyss between them.

Jenny closed her eyes and inhaled the scent of Matt's masculine cologne on the pillowcase. The time would soon come when she would have to confront the question of whether her attraction to Matt was anything more than the natural result of forcing two healthy adults to sleep in the same bedroom night after night without allowing events to follow to their natural conclusion.

Matt lay wide awake, wondering. What did Jenny want from him? Perhaps more to the point, what did he want from her? Somehow his feelings for her had passed far beyond mere sexual wanting, though that was all he'd been able to express to her. He wondered if it was possible to spend the rest of his life tied to a woman with Jenny's beliefs. He might have donned his chauvinist cloak late in life, but he wasn't sure it would be that easy to shrug it off.

Still, what she offered was tantalizing enough to make Matt begin to hope and dream again. He imagined the joyful sounds of children's laughter. He saw the faces of his sons and daughters, radiant with happiness. He smelled the musky scent of his wife after making love to her on the bed in this room. And he ached for the dream to become reality.

CHAPTER SEVENTEEN

Jenny was on a plane with Matt, bound for Houston. She fought the desire to glance at her watch. She'd expected the morning after she'd teased Matt unmercifully, then bared her soul, to be awkward and uncomfortable, but he'd made sure it wasn't. They'd taken a giant step toward real amity, which relieved some of the sexual tension. She was determined to enjoy the nine days she had left in his company without counting the minutes and hours.

"Houston strikes me as a city that should greet a feminist project with hospitality," Matt said.

"Why do you say that?"

"Isn't it the city where Billie Jean King whipped Bobby Riggs at tennis?"

Jenny laughed. "Sure, and if you think even one Texas cowboy believed before the match began that Bobby wouldn't swat Billie Jean back into the kitchen where she belonged, you're not as well-informed a chauvinist as I thought."

"I suppose you're right," Matt agreed with a chuckle. "After all, Texas is the land of good ole country boys, isn't it?"

"Not to mention roughnecks, truckers, and football," Jenny added with a wry grin.

"How did you get to Texas? And from there to New York?"

"Sam got a job offer in Houston, and we decided to live in the suburbs. I stayed there when Sam and I split up. When Melody died, I needed a change, so I decided to pursue my artistic career in the Big Apple. I was naive enough to believe I was going to wake up the world with my art."

"You haven't done such a bad job."

Jenny sensed that they were on dangerous ground and changed the focus to Matt. "What about you? How did you end up in New York?"

"Small-town boy from Iowa seeks fame and fortune—"

"No! You can't be from Iowa. You're too . . . too . . ."

"Too suave and debonair? Too good in bed?"

Jenny laughed. "The former, maybe. The latter I have no way of knowing."

"You'll have to give me a chance to prove myself one way or the other," Matt said with a predatory gleam in his eyes.

Jenny met his gaze and acknowledged that the time would come when he'd get his wish, but not until the full month of September had passed. Right now, the success of her project—and acquiring Matt's retraction—were the most important considerations.

More important than a future with Matt?

Matt hasn't offered anything.

He's offered himself.

The subject isn't even up for discussion until the project's finished.

So, which is more important, Jenny? Life or art?

Art. All right, life. Stop trying to confuse me.

Matt felt an immediate physical response to the flare of desire in Jenny's eyes. He shifted to get more comfortable.

"Something wrong?" Jenny asked.

"Don't tempt me," Matt said. "I'm trying very hard to be good."

"I'm sure you are."

Matt stared blankly at her for a moment and then groaned at her innuendo.

Jenny giggled. It was a totally feminine sound, and Matt felt his heart take a small leap in his chest. At the same time, he wondered how a relationship between them could ever work.

She would expect him to stop leaving toothpaste in the sink and to throw his undershorts in the laundry instead of on the floor. She would expect him to let her keep working even after they had children. She would expect him to do his share in the kitchen. She would want him to leave the light on at night so she could read. They didn't sound like terribly significant changes. But he knew they were only the tip of the iceberg. Marriage was all about compromise. Was he willing to make the changes necessary to find happiness with this particular woman?

"Penny for your thoughts?" Jenny said into the silence that had grown between them.

Matt smiled blandly. "I hope it's not too muggy in Houston."

"Oh." Why had she thought he might be contemplating

more weighty things—like their relationship with each other? Matt had made it clear he desired her, but he'd never said he wanted to spend his life with her. Why should he? She didn't know two people who were more unsuited to living with one another. Hadn't the past two and a half weeks proved that?

You could change.

Me? Or Matt?

Both. You can negotiate your differences.

Why should I have to change? I've been perfectly happy as I am. He's a slob; I'm neat. He's a morning person; I stay up late at nights. He expects me to wait on him; I want him to share the load.

Those are little things. He also wants children and likely will be a very good father. But I'm not going to argue with you, Jenny. The decision is up to you.

You bet it is!

It was two very solemn individuals who debarked at Houston's Hobby International Airport. But their sober moods didn't last beyond the lengthy drive in a rental car from the airport to the hotel.

"There's no such thing as a short drive in Houston," Jenny joked. "Somebody once told me an entire northeastern state could fit inside the Houston city limits." When they finally reached the hotel, Jenny was wide awake and raring to go. She wanted to do some country dancing, so she suggested, "Why don't we go to Gilley's?"

"At this hour of the night?"

"Who's watching the time? Come on, Matt, please? Believe it or not, in all the time I lived here, I never went there, even though it's a country-and-western landmark—you know, the same way most New Yorkers have never visited the Empire State Building or the Statue of Liberty. It was just too much trouble to fight the crowds to go dancing and listen to the music."

Matt held up the rope between them in exasperation. "And you pick *now* to fight the crowds?"

Jenny laughed. "It'll be fun. I know I'll never be able to get any sleep. I'm too keyed up. What do you say?"

"I say you're crazy, lady. But, why the hell not?"

At the height of its popularity, Gilley's had been a mecca for tourists, as well as a watering hole for locals. It boasted a huge dance floor and a mechanical bull that tested the patrons' balance and sobriety.

Jenny's mood was infectious, and before he'd had his second beer, Matt was laughing and tapping his foot to the fiddler's rendition of a Texas folk dance, the Cotton-eyed Joe. By the time Matt was drinking his third beer, Jenny even had him singing along to a country tune.

"Lookee here, Clete. This gent has lassoed hisself a pretty little heifer. Got her tied up good and tight."

Matt turned an amused eye toward the redneck cowboys who'd come up behind him and Jenny. The one who'd spoken had a huge lump of chewing tobacco in his cheek. Matt saw the outline of the tobacco tin in the hip pocket of the man's well-worn jeans and knew the paper cup in his hand wasn't full of soda. The cowboy set his scuffed boot on the back rung of Matt's bar stool and demanded, "Why ya got the li'l lady all tied up like that, mister?"

"None of your business," Matt replied amiably. He tipped up his beer and swallowed the cool brew.

The man called Clete sidled closer to Matt in an attempt to separate him from Jenny. "My friend Slim asked a question, mister."

"And I gave him an answer."

Jenny could see that Matt was enjoying himself. Didn't he know these rednecks were itching for a fight? While he might enjoy the brawl, he wasn't exactly free to indulge himself. "I'm ready to go, Matt."

Abruptly Slim stepped up to block Jenny's exit. "Where ya goin', honey? I ain't had a chance to dance with y'all yet."

Jenny raised herself to her full five feet nine inches and gestured to the rope that tied her to Matt. "As you can see, my man is on the possessive side. If you were to raise a finger to me, if you were to so much as breathe hard on me," she drawled, "why, I'm afraid he'd be inclined to make you very sorry."

Slim glanced quickly at Matt, as though to judge whether there was any truth behind the pretty blond woman's words.

Matt stood, and at a broad-shouldered six foot three, there was a lot of him to provide intimidation. "My woman spoke her piece. You got any more questions?"

"No, sir, I ain't," Slim said quickly. "Come on, Clete. Let's go get a beer."

As soon as the cowboys left, Jenny turned to Matt, her eyes flashing. "Just what did you think you were doing, provoking them like that? Clete had a knife hanging on his belt, and cowboys like him are always looking to draw blood."

"So you unsheathed your claws first?" Matt said with a mellow smile.

Jenny was furious at his total lack of concern. "Have you heard a word I've said?"

Matt leaned closer, nose to nose with Jenny. "I heard every single word. As a man who's *on the possessive side,* I'd say I behaved remarkably well. Never even lifted a finger to either one of those fellows," he said with a rakish grin.

"Oh. You . . . you . . . macho man!"

He laughed, his voice low and sexy, and Jenny felt a frisson of desire skitter up her spine.

Matt had once told Jenny that she was beautiful when she was angry. He hadn't changed his mind. Right now, he also found her desirable. He leaned over and whispered in her ear, "Let's go back to the hotel, Jenny. Let me hold you in my arms. I want to taste you with my lips and tongue. I want to suckle your breasts. I want to put my hands on you and inside you and make you moan with pleasure. I want to slide deep inside you and make us one. Let me love you, Jenny. Come back—"

"Matt, please stop." It was a cry of both denial and desire. "1 can't! Don't torture us both like this."

In a blind panic, Jenny ran.

Matt cursed the three beers that had loosened his tongue, cursed the need that drove him to speak, cursed the self-control that allowed Jenny to deny them both.

The rope stopped her, of course, but not before there was a significant crowd separating them. She struggled toward the exit, and Matt followed her as best he could, shoving people aside, countering the confusion, as people realized there was a rope entangling them with the man who was trying to get by.

Once outside, Jenny sucked in a breath of the cool, refreshing night air, then another one, before turning to confront Matt, who was only moments behind her. They walked side by side toward the rental car they'd parked in the large lot. Matt slipped inside from the passenger's side and scooted over behind the wheel, then waited for Jenny to get settled before he said, "Jenny, I apologize."

"Why should you be sorry? You weren't saying anything I haven't thought myself."

Matt hissed out a breath. "Why didn't you say something?"

"Why should I make it harder on both of us?" Jenny sought out Matt's eyes in the neon light from Gilley's. "I want you every bit as much as you want me, Matt. I have since the first day I laid eyes you. Maybe when my project is over and done with . . ." Left unsaid was *When you've printed a retraction.* "If you still feel the same way . . ."

"I want you, Jenny. I don't think that's ever going to change."

Jenny wondered if he was being honest with himself. *Ever* was a long time. She bit back the smart-alecky retort on her tongue. The less provocation she gave Matt to do something both of them would regret, the better. She wondered whether there was any more to his feelings than desire. Or could it be the stipulation for a retraction they'd agreed upon that was fueling his libido? She wished she didn't feel suspicious of his motives. But the fact was she did.

When they got back to their room, Matt got into his twin bed, turned his back on Jenny in the revealing T-shirt that drove him crazy, and muttered, "Just ignore the breasts hidden by that soft cotton and the long legs hanging out below it, and you'll be fine."

Meanwhile, Jenny was suffering through mental gymnastics of her own. What if Matt couldn't change? What if she discovered that she loved him, but couldn't stand to live with him? She knew that happened more often than people were willing to admit. Maybe the smart-alecky remark she'd avoided making earlier wasn't such a bad idea. It might help relieve the tension. She turned toward Matt and whispered, "I think your legs are kind of nice, too."

Matt half laughed, half groaned. "Jenny, have mercy. My willpower is only so strong."

"Good night, Matt. You're beautiful when you're angry."

"Trite, Jenny."

"True, Matt."

CHAPTER EIGHTEEN

The reviews in the Houston papers on Monday morning were all positive. In fact, two of them were glowing. Matt attributed that to the fact that all three critics were women. Because of Jenny's visit to the cemetery where Melody was buried, they didn't have a chance to pursue the matter until after they'd flown home. However, once they were settled in bed in Jenny's apartment that evening, he brought up the subject for discussion.

"Are you suggesting those three women critics are *gender biased?"* Jenny questioned. "And that if I'd been a man making the same presentation, the reviews would have been different?"

"If you'd been a man, you never would have made that particular presentation."

"You're not back to that 'artists paint what they know' theory, are you?" Jenny demanded.

"I'm afraid so."

"Matt, you've spent nearly three weeks with me. Are

you still on square one? Haven't you moved an inch in any direction?"

"I'll say this, Jenny. If I'm suggesting that those three women are gender biased, perhaps I'm also willing to agree that I'm gender biased as well."

Jenny blinked twice. "You are? I mean, of course you are. Gender biased, that is. I knew it when I read your review of *Woman at a Party*. Now we're making progress. Are you willing to print a retraction?"

"No, I'm not."

Jenny scooted over to the edge of her bed. "Why not?"

"I'm not convinced I was wrong."

"Of course you were wrong! You just admitted you were biased against me because I was a woman, before you ever came to see my performance. What kind of fair evaluation could you make under those circumstances?"

The hair was standing up on the back of Matt's neck. He didn't know exactly how Jenny had managed to rile him, but his good humor had vanished. "We don't live in a vacuum. A person—male or female—is never going to be completely neutral."

"Then I'd settle for having you admit that your review reflected a sexual bias."

"I'll just bet you would."

"You unreasonable, stubborn—"

"Can it, Jenny."

Jenny leapt off the bed and paced back and forth the length of her tether, her temper simmering.

Every time she turned, the tail of her T-shirt flipped up, giving Matt an enticing glimpse of slender legs and silken underwear. Could she really be oblivious to what she was doing to him?

"What are you really angry about, Jenny? Does this little display have anything to do with the fact that I didn't take the initiative and make love to you in Houston?"

Jenny gasped and stopped dead. "That was a low blow, Matt."

"You set the rules for this game, baby. You've wiggled your cute little fanny at me one time too many."

Matt grasped the rope and began to gather it up in his hands, pulling Jenny toward him. She didn't come willingly or easily. She sat down and dug her toes into the carpet, but there was never any question of who was stronger. Slowly, but surely, Matt dragged her closer, until she was lying on the rug beside his bed, and he was standing spread-legged over her. He dropped to his knees, straddling her waist, taking care not to touch her. He leaned over her with his weight braced on his palms on either side of her head. "All right, Jenny. Ask me for what you want."

Jenny lay rigid beneath him. "I want you to retract your review."

"What else do you want?"

"Why are you doing this?"

"What else do you want?" he demanded, his voice harsh.

"Nothing, damn you!"

It took all Matt's willpower not to grab her by the shoulders and shake her. She wanted him. He knew she wanted him, yet she lay defiant beneath him, and all the more desirable because of her defiance.

"Matt . . . I . . ."

In that instant, Matt knew she was going to give him what he wanted. And he was just as sure that he'd changed his mind about wanting it. Because if he took her now, he would have her for the moment, but he would lose her for a lifetime. Abruptly, he stood and stepped away from her.

"Go to bed, Jenny."

"Matt, I—"

"Move your butt! Before I change my mind."

Jenny scrambled from the floor into her bed and yanked the covers up over her shoulders.

Matt lay down in his bed and stared at the ceiling. When he heard Jenny's muffled weeping, he closed his eyes and gritted his teeth, forcing himself to ignore it. *That woman is damned lucky. She has no reason to be crying, that's for sure. As many knots as she has me tied in, she ought to be laughing her fool head off.*

CHAPTER NINETEEN

A tug on the rope at her waist woke Jenny before dawn the next morning. She opened her eyes to the sight of Matt sitting fully dressed on the edge of his bed, staring down at her.

"I need to make a trip over to see my editor today," he announced.

"All right," Jenny said, cautiously drawing the sheet up to her neck as an extra shield against Matt's steady gaze. "After class—"

"George is waiting for me right now."

Jenny sat up in bed and shoved her hair out of her eyes. Matt looked haggard, as though he hadn't slept a wink. "Is there some emergency?"

Matt avoided Jenny's eyes as he answered, "You could say that."

"Oh."

"The cab is already waiting."

Jenny hurriedly dressed, wondering how she'd slept

soundly enough to miss a call. Or had Matt called George? After what had happened between them last night, anything was possible. A shiver of alarm traveled down her back. Surely Matt wasn't going to back out of the project at this late date. Not after they'd managed to make it through all but the last showing.

Jenny's musings were left unresolved through the early morning cab ride to the offices of *Artist's World*. When they arrived, Matt stepped inside the threshold of George's office before turning to block Jenny's way. "You can have a seat outside. I may be a while." Then he dropped the extra length of rope between them on the carpeted floor so it would pass beneath the portal, and shut the door in her face.

Jenny stood there in disbelief for a moment, then sank into the comfortable chair that had obviously been placed outside George's door for just such a purpose.

What's going on, Jenny?

I have no idea.

Do you think he's quitting?

Not without printing a retraction, he isn't!

Do you think that's why he's here to talk to George?

I don't know what to think. But if he knows what's good for him, he'd better not make me late for class.

Jenny followed the trail of rope from her waist to where it was mashed into the carpet beneath George's door. She listened for voices but couldn't hear anything beyond the wooden partition. Whatever Matt was saying, he must be saying it in a normal tone of voice. That was a good sign, wasn't it?

Half an hour later, Matt opened the door. His jaws were tight, his eyes bleak. "Let's go," he said curtly.

Jenny stood and searched out George, who appeared

momentarily in the doorway.

"Hello, Jenny," he said with a friendly smile.

"Hello, George. How are you?"

"Are you going to stand there and gab all day?" Matt demanded.

"I think he wants to go," George said, giving Jenny's hand a reassuring squeeze.

Jenny turned to Matt. "Are we in a hurry?"

"You're the one with the 9:00 a.m. class."

"I guess we do need to go. I'll see you soon, George."

"Sooner than you think," George murmured as Matt towed Jenny away.

"What did he want?" Jenny asked once they'd caught a cab and were on their way to the New School campus.

"I called him, he didn't call me," Matt said through tight jaws.

"Well, what did you want from him?"

"I wanted out!"

Jenny's face paled until her stricken eyes provided the only color in her face.

"Are you satisfied now?" Matt glared at her and thrust a hand recklessly through his shaggy black hair. "I just wanted out."

"Oh." Jenny swallowed over the huge lump in her throat. "I take it George wouldn't let you quit."

"Hell, no! He threatened me with—"

"He threatened you? With what? How?"

"He's my boss, Jenny. He's got all the power he needs to make my life miserable."

"George doesn't seem like the kind of guy who'd do that."

"You don't know George Taplinger the way I do. Take it from me, George is one tough cookie."

"So you gave in to his threats, and that's why you're still here, tied to me."

Matt sighed. "That's about it."

Jenny could make a good guess why Matt wanted out of the project. But if he thought she'd done anything to arouse him on purpose last night, he was wrong. Maybe it would be best if they just got everything out in the open.

"As long as you're stuck with me, why don't we make a clean breast of everything that's bothering us about living with each other? You tell me what you want from me, I'll tell you what I want from you, and we'll do the best we can the rest of our time together to get along. How does that sound?"

Matt stared off into the shadowed canyon created by New York's skyscrapers. He pursed his lips ruefully and glanced at her from the corner of his eye. "That doesn't sound like a half-bad idea. Who goes first?"

They'd arrived at the school, and Jenny waited until Matt had paid the driver and they were walking to her class to continue. "I'll tell you what. Let's have a picnic in Central Park this afternoon, and we'll draw straws then to see who goes first."

"You got it."

CHAPTER TWENTY

As far as Jenny was concerned, Central Park was one of New York's greatest resources. It was a haven of nature in an unnatural setting. She spread a blanket on the grass and plopped down on top of it to unload the paper bag full of goodies she and Matt had picked up at a deli on the way.

When they'd devoured the sandwiches, chips, and soda, she held up two straws and said, "Short straw goes first."

Matt chose the short straw. "Figures."

"All right. Let's hear it," Jenny said, stretching out on her side with her head held up by one hand. "What's driving you nuts about living with me?"

"You mean aside from the fact that I want to make love to you and can't?"

Jenny gulped. She was back in deep water, and she'd never been a very strong swimmer. "Aside from that."

Matt shrugged. "A lot of little things, if you want to

know the truth."

"Like what?" Jenny persisted.

"I'd like you not to nag me about leaving toothpaste in the sink."

"I don't nag."

"Do you want to hear what I have to say or not?"

Jenny sat up and ran her fingers across her lips like an imaginary zipper.

"I want the light out at a decent hour."

"One o'clock is decent."

"Some people get up early in the morning to exercise."

"All right. I'll turn out the lights at twelve-thirty," Jenny suggested.

"Eleven."

"Midnight."

"Eleven-thirty," Matt compromised.

"That's an hour and a half earlier than I normally go to bed," Jenny argued.

"I can think of something a whole lot better to do with the time than read," he growled.

"Like what?"

"Like make love to you."

"Why do you keep saying that?"

"Because it's true. The whole time you're lying there reading about some hero making love to some heroine, I'm lying there thinking about making love to you. It's damned uncomfortable."

"All right. I'll turn the light out at eleven-thirty."

"Just like that."

"Just like that. Is there anything else?" Jenny asked. "You seem to be on a roll."

"I'd . . . uh . . . I'd like you to wear something different for pajamas. Something that doesn't show off your legs."

Matt's eyes followed the length of Jenny's long legs, from her ankles to her denim-clad thighs. "I'd prefer not to have so much temptation thrust in my path at bedtime."

Jenny's mouth was dry as she met Matt's heated gaze. "All right," she croaked. "You got it."

"Your turn, Jenny. What can I do to make the next ten days easier for you?"

"Wipe out the sink. Pick up your shorts." Jenny found it hard to concentrate. Her eyes had caught on the strong pulse at Matt's throat, then drifted down to the rock-hard muscles in his chest and the strong sinews in his forearms, and finally to the ridge in the soft cotton below his belt.

"Jenny?"

"What?"

"If you want to check me out, *Ms.* Smith, all you have to do is ask."

Jenny's face flushed. "I'm sorry, Matt. What were we? Oh, yes. What did . . . I was going to ask . . . I'd be pleased if you'd stick a bag on your head and cover up those sexy gray eyes and that smug grin. At least then I could think straight."

Matt's amused chuckle at Jenny's totally flustered state soon became a full-fledged guffaw.

When the ridiculousness of her request sank in, Jenny's good humor grew to match Matt's, until they were both rolling around on the blanket laughing uncontrollably.

By the time their howls had subsided to pleased giggles, they were lying side by side on their backs. Matt shifted to his side, and Jenny gave him a playful once-over.

Matt waited until she'd finished, then smiled and said, "You're priceless, Jenny. No wonder I lo—" He cut himself off.

A tense silence ensued as they both absorbed the significance of what he'd almost said.

Jenny sat up and concentrated on straightening her blouse, which had pulled out of her waistband, exposing her abdomen. Her eyes sought out Matt's piercing gaze. The caring—and the passion—were both there. "This is crazy," she whispered.

Matt broke off a tall stem of grass and tore it into little pieces, which drifted away in the wind. "I'm not happy about the situation, either. But there it is."

"This is impossible."

"You're telling me."

"I don't know what to say."

"You don't have to say anything, Jenny. I wasn't asking whether you returned my feelings—"

"But I do." She smiled sadly. "I don't know what we're moping about. Most couples would be overjoyed to find out they have feelings for each other."

"Most couples never spend their first three weeks sleeping together in the same bedroom, forbidden to touch." Matt fingered the rope, which was looking as frayed as their tempers had become on occasion. "You do realize, Jenny, that unless we do something about it, once we cut this rope, we're likely to go in different directions and never see each other again."

Jenny swallowed past the painful lump in her throat. "Uh-huh." The only conclusion she could draw was that he might love her, but he wasn't going to let it go any further than that.

The uncomfortable silence was back.

Jenny busied herself collecting the paper bags from the deli. "The sun's about gone. I guess we should go."

They both stood and grabbed for the blanket, but Matt took it from her and shook it in the direction of the gentle breeze, before he gave it a casual folding.

"Will you be my date for the benefit on Saturday?" he asked.

"What about Rachel?"

"I want to go with you."

"I don't know if that's such a good idea."

Matt pursed his lips in thought. "Look, you have to go whether you go with me as a date or not. We might as well save the hassle of picking up and dropping off two more people."

For practical reasons, Matt's invitation made perfect sense. The problem was it increased the intimacy between them at a time when he'd made it clear that their relationship would be over in ten days' time. For her own protection, Jenny's inclination was to refuse.

Matt was watching Jenny chew her lip in indecision, so he saw the moment when she finally made up her mind to refuse him.

"I'll go with you Saturday, of course, but I don't think we should call it a date."

"If that's the way you want it, Jenny, that's the way it will be."

"That's the way I want it."

CHAPTER TWENTY-ONE

Jenny spent the next few days granting the requests Matt had made in Central Park. She wouldn't swear to it, but she thought Matt had actually thrown his undershorts in the laundry basket one morning. He hadn't been an angel, but she hadn't seen a lick of toothpaste in the sink since Tuesday. His cooperative behavior touched her more than she could say.

Jenny realized she was wishing hard for the sort of happy ending that was promised in her romance novels. Matt would suddenly become the forceful yet sensitive hero who would sweep her off her feet and carry her away to the land of Happily Ever After. But he'd given her no indication that anything like that was going to happen. He'd been friendly, fun to be with, cooperative—but distant. And George Taplinger had helped him keep that distance.

On Tuesday evening they'd barely arrived home from the park when George knocked on the door.

"I have some business to discuss with Matt," he'd said.

Jenny had invited him in, and he and Matt had sat at the kitchen table and worked. Jenny had finally fallen asleep on the couch. Matt had woken her up after George left, and they'd gone right to bed.

George's mysterious arrival immediately after the dinner hour "to discuss business" had repeated itself on Wednesday and Thursday. When Jenny turned on the TV to watch Thursday night football, all pretense of work had been dropped, and Matt and George joined her to watch the game. Once again, George stayed late, and by the time he left, Jenny and Matt dropped into bed.

Jenny began to suspect what the two men must have discussed at the office on Tuesday morning. On Friday she'd greeted George with a sardonic smile. "Hello. Here to act as guard dog again?"

George blushed, but he didn't contradict her.

Matt glared, as if daring her to say anything.

"If you'd brought your wife, we could have played some bridge. But since you didn't, why don't we play poker?" Jenny suggested.

By the end of the evening, Jenny was the big winner, with a total of forty-three toothpicks to Matt's forty-one and George's three. George had a terrible poker face, but he made a wonderful buffer. Thanks to his presence, she and Matt made it through the evening with a minimum of tension, sexual or otherwise. And they only had to last seven more days without touching for Jenny to fulfill the requirements of her project.

CHAPTER TWENTY-TWO

Late Saturday afternoon, after Jenny showered and washed her hair, she began rifling madly through her closet, trying to find something to wear to the United Way benefit. Nothing looked right.

Matt was lying on his bed, his hands clasped comfortably behind his head, watching her. "What about the one you're holding in your left hand?"

Jenny held the orange, red, and purple gown in front of her and frowned at her image in the full-length mirror behind the closet door . "I think it's a little too much."

"I vote for that dress I watched you making out of silk and velvet last week. You know. Vintage Jenny Smith Wearable Art—tons of textures, cool colors, diamonds, rubies, pearls?"

Jenny laughed and put back the two dresses she'd been holding, in order to pull out the outfit Matt had described. She'd been experimenting when she'd made it. One of her clients had asked for something daring, and Jenny had made this outfit. When she'd presented it to the client, the woman had said, "Darling, I said *daring*, not *decadent*." The client had been Jenny's size, so she'd brought it home. She hadn't foreseen actually wearing it, but it was a piece of art she'd created, so she couldn't very well throw it away, either.

Jenny held it up. "I don't know, Matt."

"Try it on."

"It doesn't have a back."

He grinned. "I won't tell. Come on. Try it on."

She disappeared behind her dressing screen and slipped out of her bathrobe and into the outfit. It fit as if it had been made for her. Jenny smiled to herself, as she tugged on the part of the gown that had probably prompted the label of *decadent*. There was a man's white dress glove sewn at a provocative angle across the bodice, so that when the dress was worn, the glove cupped the wearer's right breast. Meanwhile, the back of the dress draped from the shoulders all the way to the waist, so no bra could be worn under the velvet bodice. A full-length satin skirt hugged her from waist to ankles, but had an enticing slit up the front to a point several inches above her knees.

If feeling sexy was decadent, the dress fit her client's description, because the instant Jenny pulled the gown up over her shoulders, she felt as though Matt were touching her. Heat pooled behind the satin caressing her belly, and her nipples budded beneath the velvet that shaped her breasts.

When Jenny came out from behind the screen, Matt had to force himself to stay on the bed. Her eyes were lambent with passion, and her walk . . . Her walk said her legs were shaky, and that it would take only a little effort to put her on her back beneath him.

"That's quite an outfit, *Ms.* Smith."

"Why, thank you, Mr. Benson." Jenny walked all the way over to Matt and sat down beside him on the narrow bed.

"Whose glove is that?" he asked, reaching out with one hand to match the glove's grip, careful not to actually touch.

Jenny closed her eyes and leaned her head back, letting her hair fall down her bare back. "I wish it were yours, and that you were wearing it."

Matt jerked his hand away as though he'd been scalded and quickly slipped off the bed on the side opposite Jenny. "If you could bottle whatever that dress does for a woman, you'd make a fortune," he said dryly. "I assume you've decided to wear it tonight."

Jenny curled up like a kitten facing him and said with a feline smile, "I think I will."

"If you don't mind, I'll take my shower now," Matt said. He made a hasty exit, closing the bathroom door firmly between them. He used the entire time he was showering to preach a lesson in good behavior to his libido. It was a totally wasted effort.

The instant he stepped out of the bathroom, he was assailed by the scent of expensive perfume. Jenny was sitting with her back to him, and he was treated to the lovely sight of her bare back draped in dark blue velvet. He followed the indentation of her spine to the point where soft, clinging fabric thwarted his view.

At that moment, Jenny turned and smiled at him. She'd been at work on her makeup, and the innocent, wide-spaced blue eyes that had first attracted him to her now looked sultry. Bright red lipstick outlined her lips in a pout, and gloss gave them a wet look. Her cheekbones had never appeared so high and proud. Her shoulder-length hair hung free, and the silky, golden mass floated around her shoulders, begging to be touched. In fact, everything about her begged to be touched. He grabbed his tuxedo and retreated into the steamy bathroom.

Jenny was so focused on getting her makeup just right, that she was surprised when she finally turned around to discover that Matt was standing behind her wearing his tuxedo. The contrast of the stark white shirt with his tanned skin, and the perfect fit of the coat and black trousers simply made him look powerfully attractive.

She stood and said, "That's quite an outfit."

Matt ate her up with his eyes. He knew that if they didn't leave, he would have that dress off her in the next two seconds. "Come on, Jenny. We'd better get going."

Jenny felt the sharp sexual need arcing between them and felt the temptation to do something about it, but in the end, she turned in a swirl of satin and led the way out the door.

They made an impressive couple when they arrived at the hotel hosting the banquet. Matt had arranged to have his art supplies and easel set up earlier in the afternoon, and he promptly took his place on the low camp stool behind the easel and left Jenny to her own devices. Almost immediately, one of the art patrons attending the benefit occupied the long-legged director's chair across from Matt and asked for a caricature.

Jenny stood at Matt's shoulder and watched in awe as an exaggerated version of the woman's features took form. Jenny marveled that he could work so quickly and effectively. In this case, he focused on the woman's hairdo and her smile. Both were already flamboyant, but Matt's charcoal drawing presented them in comical dimensions.

"Who does your hair?" he asked the woman.

"Simone's," she answered.

"You should ask her to put a little more curl in it next time," he said earnestly.

The woman laughed, since frizzy auburn curls were dripping off her head in clumps, like hanging wisteria blossoms.

When Matt was finished, there were chuckles and murmurs of approval from the crowd that had gathered, and the director's chair was quickly filled with another charity patron.

He worked until midnight without a break. Having his hands busy kept him from smoking, but Jenny occasionally intercepted a glass of champagne from a passing tray and offered it to him. Again, because he needed both hands to work, he only took a sip before setting it aside. Jenny would finish the rest of the glass and grab another, when she thought he might be thirsty again.

He was more than just a good artist, she thought as she watched him draw for hour after hour. He had a way with people. Most left after five minutes in the director's chair with a smile on their faces, having happily parted with their one-hundred-dollar donation in exchange for a signed Matt Benson caricature.

Just before he was ready to quit for the evening, he coaxed Jenny into the chair. "Come on, Jenny. I want to do you."

"I don't have your sitting fee with me," Jenny demurred.

"I'll donate it. Come on. Please sit for me."

Several of the patrons, including George Taplinger

and his wife, urged her to comply. Laughing helplessly, she finally gave in. She couldn't imagine which of her features Matt would choose to exaggerate, but from the Cheshire-cat grins on the faces of those who were watching him work, she wasn't going to be disappointed.

When Matt finished, he signed his name with a flourish and said, "You can look now."

Jenny was almost afraid to see how Matt perceived her, but because people were watching, she had no choice. Like Matt's other patrons, Jenny was pleased by his whimsy. He'd made her eyes huge and sparkling with mischief; her breasts were full, and lovingly cupped by the white glove on her dress; and her legs were so long and gangly that from her waist down she could have passed for a giraffe.

Matt had been drawing for so many hours that he'd penned the full-length caricature of Jenny almost on reflex. When he stood back and looked at what he'd produced, he was stunned. He'd drawn a caricature, all right. There, preserved for posterity, was the stereotypical Matt Benson date—big-eyed, full-busted and long-legged. But Jenny was so much more than that!

Matt exchanged a quick look with George and knew that even if Jenny hadn't seen it, his boss had recognized the drawing for what it was.

"Jenny, I'll draw another one if you want. I'm so tired, I guess I—"

"No, Matt, it's perfect. You have a great eye and a vivid imagination. I don't know how you've lasted this long without collapsing."

Relieved that Jenny wasn't offended, he unbent enough to admit, "I'm beat. What do you say we head home?"

They said their goodbyes to George and his wife, as well as to the chairman of the benefit, who thanked Matt profusely for the contribution of his time and talent. Then they were on their way home in the limo Matt had rented for the occasion.

Jenny settled back on the comfortable leather seat and closed her eyes.

"You look tired, too," Matt said.

Jenny peered up from beneath lowered lashes, and her lips curved in a lazy smile. "Not really. But I think I may have had too much champagne. I seem to have this sort of—I don't know how to describe it—devil-may-care attitude tonight."

Matt swore under his breath. "Jenny, don't do this to me."

The lazy smile broadened, and the lashes swept lower. "Don't worry, Matt. You're safe."

At least until we get back to my apartment.

CHAPTER TWENTY-THREE

"What are you doing, Jenny?"

"I'm undressing."

"Then get behind the screen."

"No."

Matt knew he was in trouble. Disaster was staring him in the face. He tried to ignore her, but that was impossible under the circumstances. He was at the end of his rope. Unfortunately, Jenny was at the other end.

He watched as she slid the shoulders off the dress and let it drop, revealing a lacy garter belt, silk stockings and skimpy bikini panties—all black as sin and twice as sexy.

She turned to face him wearing only the provocative feminine undergarments.

Matt swallowed hard.

Jenny took one step toward him, then another.

"Stop right there," Matt said, holding out a hand like a traffic cop. "You've had a little too much champagne, and I don't want you doing something tonight you'll regret tomorrow."

Jenny smiled a predatory smile. "I know perfectly well what I'm doing. As to whether or not I'll have any regrets tomorrow . . . I'm counting on you to make sure I don't." She took another step closer. Only inches separated them now.

Matt's senses were tuned in to the feminine signals Jenny was sending: the sexy droop of her eyelids, the pout of her lower lip, her upthrust breasts, the jut of her hipbones, and her wide-legged stance all combined to form an irresistible siren's call he was helpless to resist.

"There won't be any retraction, Jenny," he said, his voice harsh with need. "I want that understood now, before we go any further."

A shadow passed across Jenny's eyes, then disappeared. "No retraction. Fine. Now, can we put all that behind us and do what we've both been aching to do for nearly a month?"

Matt could hardly believe his ears. Jenny aching? For him? He had to clear his throat to say, "Tell me what you want."

"I want you, Matt. Touching me. Loving me. Deep, deep inside me." Jenny's eyes never left Matt's, as she lifted her hands to slip off his jacket and loosen his tie. Then she reached for the top stud of his shirt and removed it.

Well, you've done it now, Jenny. You *touched* him *before the thirty days were up.*

This was inevitable.

Excuses, excuses.

I love him.

What about your project, Jenny?

I'm busy right now. Talk to me tomorrow.

Jenny's hands were trembling as she removed the rest

of the studs. When Matt reached up to help her, she captured his wrists and said, "I want to do it."

Although his body was taut with desire, Matt stood perfectly still while Jenny removed his cummerbund, then slowly pulled the shirt from his trousers. When she was done, she slid both hands inside the opening she'd created and let her fingers test the muscled ridges of his chest and belly. She then shoved the starched white cotton shirt off his shoulders so she could look her fill. She leaned across the narrow distance that separated her from Matt to take one budding male nipple into her mouth and suck on it.

Matt groaned as the feel of Jenny's lips on his skin broke his control. He did what he'd imagined doing all evening. He fitted the imprint of his hand where the white glove that cupped Jenny's right breast had rested all evening. Jenny arched upward to meet his touch on her naked flesh. With his other hand Matt pulled her hips into the cradle of his own, until their bodies, too, fit hand-in-glove. He thrust once against her, letting her feel the strength of his need.

Matt found Jenny's mouth and bit at the pouting lower lip that had so tantalized him over the past three weeks. He teased the soft underside of her upper lip with his tongue and then dipped inside, enticing her to meet him halfway, before tasting her fully.

Jenny met Matt's ardor and matched it with her own. Her hips curved into his, finding pleasure and seeking more. Her hands worked their way from his chest to his shoulders and sieved into his hair. She pulled his head down so she could reach his mouth more easily.

"I like the way you kiss," Matt said, as his lips drifted across Jenny's chin and down her throat. "Lots of little nibbles."

Jenny laughed. "You kiss kind of nibbly yourself."

"That's because you taste good," Matt murmured against her skin.

She tilted her head to give him better access to her neck, then shivered as his teeth nipped at her earlobe and his moist breath filled her ear. "I knew it would be like this," she murmured.

"Like what?"

"My heart is pounding so hard, it feels like it's going to burst."

Matt grinned and admitted, "Mine too. Here, feel." He took one of Jenny's hands and laid it against his chest where his heart beat hard beneath flesh and bone. He stood back so he could see her eyes. They were lambent with need, shining with happiness. "It's time for bed, Jenny."

Jenny felt her heart, which she'd thought was already at a full gallop, take off for the races. "I was planning to read a little," she said with a laugh.

"I'd like to suggest something better we can do."

"Better than reading?"

The sound of Jenny's throaty voice sent a fierce shaft of desire arrowing to Matt's loins. He pulled Jenny into his embrace, placing her arms around his neck. His hands roamed the bare expanse of her back, pressing her naked breasts against his chest. His mouth roamed her throat and teased her earlobes, as his hands found their way to her buttocks before slipping inside her silky panties and bringing her belly to meet his.

Jenny's whole body was awash with sensation. She sought Matt's skin with her mouth, returning the delight he offered her, only to discover that kissing Matt fed her own pleasure.

Matt whispered in her ear, "You're so beautiful, Jenny." He bent his head and slid his tongue around the edge of a nipple, then sucked it into his mouth.

Jenny grabbed a handful of his silky hair, holding him there. "You make me feel . . . so much. I never imagined . . ."

He pleasured her, teasing and taunting, until Jenny was breathless with desire. She returned the favor, laughing and playing with him. He made a game of removing her black silk stockings, kissing his way down each leg to her foot. Then he unfastened the garter belt and skimmed it away. She was so bound up in touching him that it took a moment before she realized he'd removed her panties as well. Jenny grasped Matt's shoulders as his hands slid down her belly to the tops of her thighs and back up to the nest of curls that sheltered her femininity. For an instant she held her legs together, barring his way.

"Jenny, love, let me in," he coaxed.

His hands were gentle as they circled her concave belly, found her hipbones and then headed back again to the core of her. Jenny widened her stance slightly, and Matt's hand found what it sought.

She let her head fall back as she surrendered to his touch. His mouth found her breast again, and the combination of sensations took her breath away. "That . . . feels . . . so good."

She wanted more. Needed more.

Feverishly, Jenny's hands fumbled at the zipper of Matt's trousers. She had his pants halfway down his hips before he managed to stop her. "Jenny, wait."

"I can't wait. I want you inside me. Now."

Matt didn't argue. He simply helped her finish

undressing him, then yanked the covers off his bed. He lifted her into his arms and laid her down, coming to rest on top of her. "This is where you belong," he said. "This is where you've always belonged."

His mouth captured Jenny's, stopping any protest she might have made. He spread her legs with his thighs and thrust into her.

Jenny surged upward to meet him, until he was lodged deep inside.

Matt paused and raised himself on his arms. He brushed aside the sweaty curls on her forehead and said, "I'm yours. Do with me what you will."

"I think you have that backwards," she said with a soft laugh, "But if my wish is your command, I'd like you to keep on doing what you're doing."

Matt chuckled. He backed away slightly and thrust again. "How's that?"

She slipped a hand from his buttocks down between his thighs, and he thrust again deeper, harder.

Jenny wrapped her legs around Matt and held on through the tumultuous lovemaking that followed.

There was no more talking, no more laughing, no more thinking, only pleasurable moans and whispered words without meaning. At long last, sweating and sated, they clung to one another, attempting to regather lost wits and to quiet racing heartbeats.

Matt rolled to his side, bringing Jenny with him. She pressed herself against him, not wanting to be separated.

He pulled the sheet up over them, then reached over and turned off the light. He tightened his hold on her and said, "What happens now?"

"I don't know," she whispered. "I really don't know."

In another moment, Matt was asleep.

Jenny lay there wide awake, uncomfortable because the knot in the rope that circled her waist and still bound them together had slipped around between them. She tugged at it until she was comfortable, then settled her head on Matt's shoulder and one arm across his chest.

During the night, his hold on her loosened, and she turned onto her side away from him. She closed her eyes in despair, lying awake in the quiet darkness until sleep finally claimed her.

CHAPTER TWENTY-FOUR

When Jenny woke in the morning, she found that Matt had settled a possessive arm around her waist and pulled her into his embrace, so her buttocks nestled against him.

"Good morning, sleepyhead," he murmured in her ear.

He tightened his hold, and Jenny realized that he was hard and ready. "I've heard of starting the day with a bang," she quipped, "but this is ridiculous."

Matt laughed, his voice rough with need. "It should be no surprise that I want you again."

Jenny closed her eyes and sighed. "I want you, too, Matt, but I think we have some talking to do first."

She tried to free herself, but he held her snug against him. "There's no reason why we can't talk like this."

"I want to see your face."

He hesitated a moment, then released her. "All right. Let's talk."

Jenny scooted off the bed and retrieved her robe from the bathroom door. Matt settled for arranging the sheet at his waist. She returned and sat at the foot of his bed.

The two of them simply looked at each other for a moment.

"Did you get any sleep at all?" Matt said at last.

"I couldn't fall asleep after . . . I couldn't sleep."

"Do you have regrets about what happened between us last night?"

Jenny fiddled with the length of frayed rope that lay on the tangled sheets. She opened her mouth to speak, then closed it again. At last she said, "I'll have to call and cancel the showing of *Separate but Equal* that was scheduled for this afternoon at the gallery in Soho."

"I don't see why. We never untied the rope between us."

"But we didn't keep ourselves separated for the full thirty days. My project—"

"Your project aimed to prove that a man and a woman could be more to one another than sexual objects. What happened between us last night doesn't disprove that theory, it only reinforces it."

"I don't see how you can say that."

Matt closed the distance between them, grasping Jenny by the shoulders and looking into her eyes. "I can say that because I love you. You're much more to me than simply a sexy woman, Jenny. Although you are pretty sexy." He gave her a quick, hard kiss on the mouth. "You proved what you wanted to prove. Believe it."

She looked down at her hands, which were still twisting the frayed cord. "All right, Matt. I'll hold the showing this afternoon, because I can see that at this point it would do my career more harm than good to cancel it. I've lost enough credibility with the New York art community as it is."

Jenny left unsaid the fact that there would be no retraction to improve her reputation. Yet she felt no regret for what she'd done. After all, life was more important than art, and the promise of a lifetime with Matt was well worth the sacrifice of the few days left of *Separate but Equal*. She gently shook herself free of Matt's grasp. "Are you still planning to write a review of the performance here in New York?"

"I'll have to write something, Jenny." He tried to soften the effect of his words by explaining, "George would have my head if he didn't get his article, after letting me have all this time off from work."

"Then I think it would be better if we didn't see each other after the performance this afternoon, until that obligation is fulfilled. I'll cut the rope when the performance is done, and we can go our separate ways."

Matt started to argue, but Jenny interrupted. "You can hardly expect to write a fair, impartial article if we're living together as lovers, and if we stay together for the next five days, you know that's inevitable." She set a hand on Matt's arm. "Do what you have to do. Then we can see if what we seem to have found is really there, or if it's only an illusion that fades, once we're not forced to remain in each other's company."

"It's no illusion, Jenny."

"I hope not, Matt." She chewed her lower lip for another moment before she asked, "Have you thought about what it would be like to spend the rest of your life living with me?"

Matt's gray eyes skipped away from her intense perusal. "We have some problems that have to be worked out. Every couple does."

When Jenny snorted, Matt met her gaze and said, "There's no reason why we can't resolve the differences between us. That is, if we're both willing."

"I'm willing," Jenny said with a wry smile. "I don't want to miss the chance of seeing a chauvinist and a feminist settle down to live Happily Ever After."

"We have more in common than you think."

"Like what?"

"We each have a failed marriage in our past, with a partner who was wrong for us. We both want children. We both love art. We . . ." Matt searched for another significant similarity. "We both love football," he said at last.

Jenny laughed.

"Don't laugh. Think of all those football widows."

"And widowers," Jenny inserted.

"And widowers," Matt dutifully repeated. "We won't ever have to worry about spending Mondays, Thursdays, and Sundays alone during football season."

"You're grasping at straws."

"I'm fighting for my life."

Jenny's features sobered. "Oh, Matt." She threw herself into his arms, no longer able to stand the separation she was forcing between them.

Matt tightened his arms around her. He'd write the damned review for George, and then he'd come back to claim his woman. He knew he'd sound like a caveman, if he explained that to Jenny, so he didn't say anything. She would find out soon enough that he had no intention of letting her go. If he had anything to say about it, the chauvinist pig and the feminist prig were going to become man and wife.

CHAPTER TWENTY-FIVE

"This collection of photographs is incredible, Patrick," Jenny said, as she perused the digital pictures recording her project. "I'd forgotten about that time Matt and I took a carriage ride through Central Park. And this one, with Matt working at his desk at *Artist's World*. I don't remember you taking it."

"You were asleep on the couch in his office," Patrick explained.

"Oh."

"Have you heard from him, Jenny?"

"Not for the past week. Not since I cut the rope."

"Why don't you call him?"

Jenny excused Patrick's intrusion into her personal life. After all, they'd certainly become more than a little familiar, thanks to their spontaneous date. In addition, she and Matt had seen Patrick often over the nearly four weeks of her project, as he'd recorded various moments with his camera. Jenny scanned the photographs until she reached the one that showed her cutting her way through the rope with a pocketknife. She'd insisted on calling Patrick to record the moment, even though they were five days short of spending the entire thirty days together.

Matt hadn't taken his eyes off her, and once the rope was cut, he'd taken her in his arms and held her. Just held her. Jenny hadn't wanted him to let her go. She moved to the next photograph, and there it was, in vivid color, the two of them as close as two people could be. Why hadn't he called?

"This week's copy of *Artist's World* should be on the stands by now. Would you like me to go out and get one for you?"

It took the touch of Patrick's hand on her shoulder to make Jenny aware that he was talking to her. "What did you say?"

"I'm going out to get a copy of *Artist's World*. I'll be back in a flash. Don't go away."

Jenny sat on her couch and stared out the window of her apartment.

Well, Jenny, this is it.

I thought I told you to go away.

No more hiding. No more wondering. No more waiting.

I wasn't hiding.

Sure looks like it from where I stand. Why don't you call him?

Women don't call men.

That's a sexist remark, Jenny, and unworthy of you.

Get lost.

Patrick was back too soon for Jenny's comfort. He handed Jenny the magazine. "Here it is, Jenny. The review starts on page five. I think you're going to want to read it alone, so I'll be leaving.

There was nothing on Patrick's face to tell her whether the review was good or bad, but she took it as a bad sign that he wasn't hanging around to catch her reaction. Before she could protest that she didn't want to be alone at a time like this, he'd collected his camera and his photographs and left her apartment.

CHAPTER TWENTY-SIX

"I'm here to see Matthew Benson."

The *Artist's World* receptionist had seen Jenny often enough to know who she was. "Ms. Smith. Um, it's nice to see you. I'm sorry, unless you have an appointment—"

"He'll see me. Call him."

The receptionist looked over her shoulder across the roomful of computers toward Matt's office. "He's still talking with Mr. Taplinger."

"There's a chair outside George's office. I'll wait for him there," Jenny said.

"But you can't—"

Jenny was past the receptionist before the woman could stop her. The receptionist started to call Matt and warn him that Jenny was on the way, but at that moment, two phone lines rang, and she picked one of those up instead.

Jenny made her way to George's office. She slipped

into the comfortable chair outside his door and crossed her legs to wait. That was when she realized the door wasn't closed. She didn't mean to eavesdrop, but it was hard not to hear everything they said.

"That was a great article you wrote on Jenny Smith," George said. "Worth every penny it cost me to have you gone for nearly a month. And that was some fancy footwork you did, fixing it so we didn't have to print a retraction."

"Jenny's in love with me."

"You told me a feminist prig like Jenny Smith wouldn't last ten seconds if she were tied to the right man. I guess you turned out to be the right man."

"It was a little longer than ten seconds, George."

Jenny stuck her fist in her mouth to keep from crying out. How dare he! How dare he reduce their relationship to some cheap seduction?

"About my relationship with Jenny . . ." Matt said.

"What about it?"

Jenny didn't wait to hear Matt's response. She jumped up from her chair and burst into George's office. "You don't have to say another word," she said to Matt. She turned to George and continued, "I thought you were a nice man. I can see Matt was right. You're one tough cookie, all right—an honest to God crumb! As for you—" She whirled and poked her forefinger against Matt's chest. "You are the lowest worm, the slinkiest snake, and the stinkiest stinker it has ever been my misfortune to love!"

She spun to face George again. "I'm sure a man of your editorial caliber will want to give me equal time to express my opinion of the days I spent tied to Matt Benson. Send a photographer to my apartment in an hour. I'll have a piece of performance art ready for him to shoot."

She was too furious to cry. The crying didn't come until she was on the subway home. How could she have been so wrong about Matt? After she'd read his review of *Separate but Equal,* she'd been so sure he'd changed. But it had all been lies. She practically ran from the subway to her apartment. Just wait. She'd show the whole world what Matthew Benson was really like.

Jenny gathered the materials she needed to present *Woman in her Natural State,* made the appropriate changes in her costume, and sat down in the living room to wait for the photographer to arrive.

She'd barely gotten comfortable when the knock came. She undid the last lock and opened the door to find Matt standing on the other side.

"You weren't expecting me?" he asked when he saw her stunned expression.

She tried slamming the door in his face, but he stuck his foot inside. There was no contest. In another moment he was inside the apartment, with the door closed behind him.

"What the hell are you doing opening the door to some stranger dressed like that?" he demanded. "At least you've got something in your hand you can use to protect yourself."

"I happen to be dressed in a costume," Jenny snarled. "And this—" she held up the steam iron in her hand "—is part of my performance art project."

Matt took the time to really look at what she was wearing. The black negligee wasn't quite see-through, but it skimmed the margin of decency. At her waist, she'd tied a filmy red apron. In her right hand she held an iron, and in her left hand a spatula. "What do you call this—outfit?" Matt demanded.

"This is *Woman in her Natural State.*"

Matt burst out laughing. "That's good, Jenny. Really funny."

"I wasn't trying to be funny," she snapped. "I was trying to show the world how Matt Benson perceives the female sex."

"Then you'd better get it right," he retorted.

Before Jenny could say another word, Matt had scooped her up in his arms and carried her into the bedroom. He dumped her onto the bed that had been his and stretched out on top of her, holding her down with his weight. "*Now* you have *Woman in her Natural State.* This is where you belong. In my bed."

"You chauvinist jerk!"

"How can you call me a name like that after all the *liberated* things I wrote in my review of your project?"

"All I had to do was listen at the door when you talked to George."

"When *I* talked to *George?* I didn't say a damned thing. George was doing all the talking. And what were you doing listening at the door, anyway?"

"I was there to thank you for your *kind* review. If I'd only known what you really think! What was that review, Matt? A salve for your conscience? You ruined my project—"

"*I* ruined your project?" Matt asked incredulously. "Just who seduced whom?"

"I heard George saying you didn't believe I'd last ten seconds with the right man," she said choking back a sob.

"You lasted a hell of a lot longer than that, as you very well know."

"You said there were things you wanted to tell him about our relationship. How could you, Matt? How could you tell him—"

Matt ended her tirade by capturing her mouth with his. Jenny didn't make it easy. She fought him, and of course, he'd forgotten about the iron.

Unfortunately Jenny had too, so when she started slapping at Matt's head and shoulders she accidentally hit him with the iron, half-stunning him. She dropped the iron and spatula on the floor and reached up to frame his face with her palms. She looked deeply into his dazed eyes to see whether she'd caused a concussion. "Oh, Matt, I'm sorry. Are you all right? I didn't mean to hurt you."

Matt groaned and dropped his head on Jenny's breast. His head hurt, but it was well worth the pain to have Jenny concerned about him again. Somehow she'd overheard his conversation with George and misconstrued the whole thing.

"Jenny?"

"What, Matt?"

"You interrupted me in George's office a moment too soon."

"Matt, I—"

He kissed her again.

This time Jenny didn't fight him. It couldn't be good for a man with a concussion to engage in a fight.

The next time Matt came up for air, he put a fingertip across Jenny's mouth to keep her silent and said, "I was about to tell George that not only did you love me, but that I loved you, and that I planned to ask you to marry me."

Jenny grabbed Matt's finger. "You were? You do? You are?"

"I love you, Jenny. Will you marry me?"

"Yes. Oh, yes!"

They lay there grinning at each other for several moments, before it occurred to either of them that he'd just tied himself for life to an unrepentant feminist.

"Is this going to work?" Jenny asked, voicing her doubts. "Are we going to be happy together?"

He brushed a wisp of hair from her forehead. "There are never any guarantees in life, but we have a lot going for us. We can do whatever we make up our minds to do."

"I think we should work on something else right now," she said.

"What's that?"

"*Woman in her Natural State.*"

"Oh, yes. Where were we?"

"You said my place was here, in bed."

"And I was right, of course. The husband is always right, Jenny. If you'd just learn that lesson—"

He laughed when Jenny chucked him in the ribs. "Did you like the review?"

"It explained a lot about how you were feeling, what you were thinking, things I guess it was easier to write than to say."

Matt quoted into her ear, "Women aren't only angel food cake, they're also meat and potatoes. To treat a woman as no more than dessert is to miss having a full meal."

Jenny grinned. "That was the nicest food metaphor you've ever written." She caressed his shoulders, then let her hands drift down the curve of his spine. "The part I liked best was where you said that I might currently be a liberated woman, but you were hoping I'd get shackled soon."

Matt brushed the edge of his hand across Jenny's breast and watched her nipple peak beneath the negligee. She blushed, and their eyes met with a warmth that made him tremble.

"I have a piece of performance art I'd like to work on with you," he said.

Jenny tilted her hips up to meet his thrust. "What did you have in mind?"

"How about something like, *And Baby Makes Three?"*

Jenny smiled. "That sounds fine. That sounds wonderful. That sounds—"

Matt closed her mouth with a kiss.

Continue reading for a letter from the author.

Dear Reader,

The book you've just read was published in 1988 as my very first short contemporary novel, *Fit to be Tied.* I've retitled it *Something New* and updated it so the characters have cell phones and print their airline tickets on-line, but I've left the topic—feminism vs. chauvinism—as it was. Although a great deal has changed in the intervening years, I believe the novel still has something to say to the contemporary woman.

It was fascinating for me to see how far I've come as an author since I wrote those early books. It seems amazing to me that I just finished novel #57, *Blackthorne's Bride.* It's the fourth book in my historical Mail-Order Bride series, which also includes my *New York Times* bestselling novels *Texas Bride, Wyoming Bride,* and *Montana Bride.* The series follows the lives of a family of orphans who become mail-order brides to survive in the West.

I have a dozen more short contemporary novels available as e-books for you to read, all part of my popular, *New York Times* bestselling western Hawk's Way series. Each novel has the preface Hawk's Way: and the name of the various heroes. Included are: *Hawk's Way: Jesse, Hawk's Way: Adam, Hawk's Way: Faron, Hawk's Way: Garth, Hawk's Way: Carter, Hawk's Way: Dallas, Hawk's Way: Falcon, Hawk's Way Billy, Hawk's Way Mac,* and *Hawk's Way Colt.* You can order any one or all of these books from my website, www.joanjohnston.com. You'll also find a family tree on my website, to let you know in which order the books were written, and are best read.

Of course, my full-length contemporary westerns, including my Bitter Creek series, which began with *The Cowboy, The Texan,* and *The Loner*, are available either in paper or as e-books. You can also order them from my website. Be sure to sign up for my e-newsletter at my website to receive monthly updates on new releases and to enter contests.

I love hearing your comments and suggestions. You can catch up with me on Facebook at Facebook.com/joanjohnstonauthor, where I feature my table settings for my monthly dinner parties, or tweet me @joanjohnston.

Take care and happy reading,
Joan Johnston

Manufactured by Amazon.ca
Acheson, AB

33556168R00101